BLACK BEAUTY

BLACK BEAUTY

by

ANNA SEWELL

This impression first published in 1974
This edition published 1993 by
Diamond Books
77-85 Fulham Palace Road
Hammersmith, London, W6 8JB

CONTENTS

CONTENTS

CHAPTER ONE

MY EARLY HOME

THE first place that I can well remember, was a large, pleasant meadow with a pond of clear water in it. Some trees overshadowed the pond, and rushes and water-lilies grew at the deep end. Over the hedge on one side we looked into a ploughed field; and on the other we looked over a gate at our master's house which stood by the roadside. At the top of the meadow was a plantation of fir-trees; and at the bottom, a running brook overhung by a steep bank.

Whilst I was young I lived upon my mother's milk, as I could not eat grass. In the daytime I ran by her side, and at night I lay down close by her. When it was hot, we used to stand by the pond in the shade of the trees; and when it was cold, we had a nice warm shed near the plantation.

As soon as I was old enough to eat grass, my mother used to go out to work in the daytime, and to come back in the evening.

There were six young colts in the meadow besides me. They were older than I was; some were nearly as large as grown-up horses. I used to run with them, and have great fun. We used to gallop all together round and round the field, as hard as we could go. Sometimes we had rather rough play, for they would frequently bite and kick as well as gallop.

One day when there was a good deal of kicking, my mother whinnied to me to come to her; and then she said: 'I wish you to pay attention to what I am going to say to you. The colts who live here are very good colts, but they are cart-horse colts, and, of course, they have not learned good manners.

'You have been well bred and well born; your father has a great name in these parts, and your grandfather twice won the Cup at the Newmarket races; your grandmother had the sweetest temper of any horse I ever knew, and I think you have never seen me kick or bite.

'I hope you will grow up gentle and good, and never learn bad ways. Do your work with a good will; lift up your feet well when you trot, and never bite or kick even in play.'

I have never forgotten my mother's advice; I knew she was a wise old horse, and our master thought a great deal of her. Her name was Duchess, but he often called her Pet.

Our master was a good, kind man. He gave us good food, good lodging, and kind words; and he spoke as kindly to us as he did to his little children. We were all fond of him, and my mother loved him very much. When she saw him at the gate, she would neigh with joy, and trot up to him. He would pat and stroke her and say, 'Well, old Pet! How is your little Darkie?' I was a dull black, so he called me Darkie.

Then he would give me a piece of bread, which was very good, and sometimes he brought a carrot for my mother. All the horses would come to him, but I think we were his favourites. My mother always took him to the town on a market day in a light gig.

There was a ploughboy, Dick, who sometimes came into our field to pluck blackberries from the hedge. When he had eaten all he wanted he would have, what he called, fun with the colts, throwing sticks and stones at them to make them gallop. We did not much mind him, for we could gallop off; but sometimes a stone would hit and hurt us.

One day he was at this game, and did not know that the master was in the next field; but he was there, watching what was going on. Over the hedge he jumped in a moment, and catching Dick by the arm, gave him such a box on the ear as made him roar with pain. As soon as we saw the master, we trotted up nearer to see what was going on.

'Bad boy!' he said, 'bad boy! to chase the colts. This is not the first time nor the second, but it shall be the last. There, take your money and go home; I shall not want you on my farm again.' So we never saw Dick again.

Old Daniel, the man who looked after the horses, was just as gentle as our master, so we were well off.

CHAPTER TWO

THE HUNT

BEFORE I was two years old, a circumstance happened which I have never forgotten.

It was early in the spring; there had been a little frost in the night, and a light mist still hung over the plantations and meadows.

The other colts and I were feeding in the lower part of the field when we heard, quite in the distance, what sounded like the cry of dogs.

The oldest of the colts raised his head, pricked up his ears, and said, 'There are the hounds!' and immediately cantered off, followed by the rest of us, to the upper part of the field, where we could look over the hedge and see several fields beyond. My mother and an old riding horse of our master were also standing near, and seemed to know all about it.

'They have found a hare,' said my mother; 'and if they come this way, we shall see the hunt.'

Soon the dogs were all tearing down the fields of young wheat next to our meadow. I never heard such a noise as they made. They did not bark, nor howl, nor whine, but kept up a 'Yo! yo, o, o! Yo! yo, o, o! at the top of their voices. After them came a number of men on horseback, some of them in green coats, all galloping as fast as they could.

The old horse snorted and looked eagerly after them; and we young colts wanted to be galloping with them, but they were soon away into the fields lower down. Here it seemed as if they had come to a stand; the dogs left off barking, and ran about in every direction with their noses to the ground.

'They have lost the scent,' said the old horse; 'perhaps the hare will get off.'

'What hare?' I said.

'Oh! I don't know *what* hare; possibly it may be one of our

13

own hares out of the plantation. Any hare they can find will do for the dogs and men to run after.'

Before long the dogs began their 'Yo! yo, o, o!' again; and back they came all together at full speed, making straight for our meadow at the part where the high bank and hedge overhung the brook.

'Now we shall see the hare,' said my mother; and just then a hare, wild with fright, rushed by, and made for the plantation. On came the dogs, followed by the huntsmen. The dogs burst through the bank, leaped the stream, and came dashing across the field. Six or eight men leaped their horses clean over the hedge and stream, following close upon the dogs. The hare tried to get through the fence; but it was too thick, and she turned sharp round to make for the road.

Alas! it was too late; the dogs were upon her with their wild cries. We heard one shriek, and that was the end of her. One of the huntsmen rode up and whipped off the dogs, who would soon have torn her to pieces. He held her up by the leg, torn and bleeding; and all the gentlemen seemed well pleased.

As for me, I was so astonished that I did not at first see what was going on by the brook; but when I did look, there was a sad sight. Two fine horses were down; one was struggling in the stream, and the other was groaning on the grass. One of the riders, covered with mud, was getting out of the water; the other lay quite still.

'His neck is broken,' said my mother.

'And serve him right, too,' said one of the colts.

I thought the same, but my mother did not join with us.

'Well, no,' she said, 'you must not say that. But though I am an old horse, and have seen and heard a great deal, I never yet could make out why men are so fond of this sport. They often hurt themselves, spoil good horses, and tear up the fields; and all this for a hare, a fox, or a stag, that they could get more easily some other way. But we are only horses, and don't understand.'

Whilst my mother was saying this we stood and looked on. Many of the riders had gone to the young man; but my master, who had been watching what was going on, was the first to raise him. His head fell back and his arms hung down, and every one looked very serious.

There was no noise now; even the dogs were quiet, and seemed to know that something was wrong. They carried him to our master's house. I heard afterwards that the young fellow was George Gordon, the Squire's only son, a fine, tall young man, and the pride of his family.

People were now riding off in all directions, to the doctor's, to the farrier's, and no doubt to Squire Gordon, to let him know about his son.

When Mr. Bond, the farrier, came to look at the black horse that lay groaning on the grass, he felt him all over and shook his head; one of the horse's legs was broken. Then some one ran to our master's house and came back with a gun. Presently there was a loud bang and a dreadful shriek, and then all was still; the black horse moved no more.

My mother seemed much troubled. She said she had known that horse for years. His name was Rob Roy; a good, bold horse with no vice in him. Afterwards she never would go to that part of the field.

Not many days after, we heard the church bell tolling for a long time; and looking over the gate we saw a long, strange, black coach covered with black cloth and drawn by black horses. After that came another, and another, and another; and all were black. Meanwhile the bell kept tolling, tolling. They were carrying young Gordon to the churchyard to bury him. He would never ride again. What they did with Rob Roy, I never knew; but 'twas all for one little hare.

CHAPTER THREE

MY BREAKING IN

I WAS now beginning to grow handsome; my coat had grown fine and soft, and was glossy black. I had one white foot, and a pretty white star on my forehead. People thought me very handsome. My master would not sell me till I was four years old; he said lads ought not to work like men, and colts ought not to work like horses till they were quite grown up.

When I was four years old, Squire Gordon came to look at me. He examined my eyes and my mouth, and felt my legs all down. Then I had to walk, trot, and gallop before him. He seemed to like me, and said, 'When he has been well broken in, he will do very well.' My master promised to break me in himself as he would not like me to be frightened or hurt; and he lost no time about it, for the next day the breaking in began.

Every one may not know what breaking in is, so I will describe it. To break in a horse is to teach it to wear a saddle and bridle, and to carry on its back a man, woman, or child; to go just the way the rider wishes, and to do so quietly. Besides this, the horse has to learn to wear a collar, a crupper, and a breeching; and he must learn to stand still whilst these are put on. Then he must be taught to have a cart or a chaise fixed behind him, so that he cannot walk or trot without dragging it after him; and he must learn to go quickly or slowly, just as his driver wishes.

He must never start at what he sees, speak to other horses, bite, kick, or have any will of his own; but must always do his master's will, even though he may be very tired or hungry.

But the worst of all is that when his harness is once on, he may neither jump for joy nor lie down for weariness. So you see this breaking in is a great thing.

Of course, I had long been used to a halter and a headstall, and to be led about in the fields and lanes quietly, but now I was to have a bit and a bridle.

My master gave me some oats as usual, and after a good deal of coaxing, he got the bit into my mouth and fixed the bridle. What a nasty thing the bit was! Those who have never had one in their mouth cannot think how bad it feels. A great piece of cold, hard steel as thick as a man's finger is pushed between your teeth and over your tongue, with the ends coming out at the corners of your mouth, and is held fast there by straps over your head, under your throat, round your nose, and under your chin; so that no way in the world can you get rid of the nasty hard thing. Bad! bad! Yes, very bad! At least I thought so; but

I knew my mother always wore one when she went out, and that all horses did when they were grown up. And so, what with my master's pats, kind words, and gentle ways, I got to wear my bit and bridle.

Next came the saddle, but that was not half so bad. My master put it on my back very gently, whilst old Daniel held my head. Then, patting and talking to me all the time, he made the girths fast under my body. I had a few oats, then I was led about for a little while; and this went on every day till I began to look for the oats and the saddle.

At length, one morning my master got on my back and rode me round the meadow on the soft grass. It certainly did feel queer; but I must say I felt rather proud to carry my master; and, as he continued to ride me a little every day, I soon became accustomed to it.

The next unpleasant business was putting on the iron shoes; that too was very hard at first. My master went with me to the smith's forge to see that I was not hurt or frightened. The blacksmith took my feet in his hand, one after the other, and cut away some of the hoof. It did not pain me, so I stood still on three legs till he had done them all. Then he took a piece of iron the shape of my foot, clapped it on, and drove some nails through the shoe quite into my hoof, so that the shoe was firmly held. My feet were very stiff and heavy, but in time I got used to it.

And now having got so far, my master went on to break me to harness; for this there were more new things to wear. First, they placed a stiff, heavy collar just on my neck, and a bridle with great side-pieces, called blinkers, against my eyes. And blinkers indeed they were, for I could not see on either side, but only straight in front of me. Next there was a small saddle with a nasty stiff strap that went right under my tail; that was the crupper. I hated the crupper—to have my long tail doubled up and poked through that strap was almost as bad as the bit. I never felt more like kicking, but of course I could not kick such a good master; and so in time I got used to everything, and could do my work as well as my mother.

I must not forget to mention one part of my training which

I have always considered a very great advantage. My master sent me for a fortnight to a neighbouring farmer who had a meadow which was skirted on one side by the railway. Here were some sheep and cows, and I was turned in amongst them.

I shall never forget the first train that ran by. I was feeding quietly near the pales which separated the meadow from the railway, when I heard a strange sound at a distance; and before I knew whence it came—with a rush and a clatter, and a puffing out of smoke, a long, black train of something flew by, and was gone almost before I could draw my breath. I turned, and galloped to the farther side of the meadow as fast as I could go; and there I stood snorting with astonishment and fear.

In the course of the day many other trains went by, some more slowly; these drew up at the station close by, and sometimes made an awful shriek and groan before they stopped. I thought it very dreadful, but the cows went on eating very quietly, and hardly raised their heads as the black, frightful thing came puffing and grinding past.

For the first few days I could not feed at peace; but as I found that this terrible creature never came into the field nor did me any harm, I began to disregard it; and very soon I cared as little about the passing of a train as the cows and sheep did.

Since then I have seen many horses much alarmed and restive at the sight or sound of a steam-engine; but thanks to my good master's care, I am as fearless at railway stations as in my own stable.

Now if any one wants to break in a young horse well, that is the way to do it.

My master often drove me in double harness with my mother because she was steady, and could teach me how to go better than a strange horse. She told me the better I behaved, the better I should be treated, and that it was wisest always to do my best to please my master. 'But,' said she, 'there are a great many kinds of men: there are good, thoughtful men like our master, that any horse may be proud to serve; but there are bad, cruel men, who never ought to have a horse or a dog to call their own. Besides these, there are a great many men foolish, vain, ignorant, and careless, who never trouble themselves to think; these spoil more horses than any one, just for want of sense. They don't mean it, but they do it for all that. I hope you will fall into good hands; but a horse never knows who may buy him, or who may drive him. It is all a chance; but still I say, "Do your best wherever you are, and keep up your good name."'

CHAPTER FOUR

BIRTWICK PARK

AT this time I used to stand in the stable, and my coat was brushed every day till it shone like a rook's wing. Early in May there came a man from Squire Gordon's who took me away to the Hall. My master said, 'Good-bye, Darkie; be a good horse, and always do your best.' I could not say 'Good-bye,' so I put my nose into his hand; he patted me kindly, and then I left my first home. As I lived some years with Squire Gordon, I may as well tell you something about the place.

Squire Gordon's park skirted the village of Birtwick. It was entered by a large iron gate, at which stood the first lodge; and then you trotted along on a smooth road between clumps of large old trees. Soon you passed another lodge and another gate, which brought you to the house and the gardens. Beyond this lay the home paddock, the old orchard, and the stables. There was accommodation for many horses and carriages; but I need only describe the stable into which I was taken. This was very roomy, with four good stalls. A large swinging window opened into the yard; this made it pleasant and airy.

The first stall was a large, square one, shut in behind with a wooden gate; the others were common stalls—good stalls, but not nearly so large. My stall had a low rack for hay and a low manger for corn; it was called a loose-box, because the horse that was put into it was not tied up, but left loose to do as he liked. It is a great thing to have a loose-box.

Into this fine box, clean, sweet, and airy, the groom put me. I never in my life was in a better box, and the sides were not so high but that I could see through the iron rails at the top all that went on.

The man gave me some very nice oats, patted me, spoke kindly, and then went away.

When I had eaten my corn, I looked round. In the stall next to mine stood a little fat, grey pony, with a thick mane and tail, a very pretty head, and a pert little nose.

Putting my head up to the iron rails at the top of my box, I said, 'How do you do? What is your name?' He turned round as far as his halter would allow, held up his head, and said: 'My name is Merrylegs. I am very handsome. I carry the young ladies on my back, and sometimes I take our mistress out in the low chair. They think a great deal of me, and so does James. Are you going to live next door to me in the box?'

'Yes,' I replied.

'Well, then,' he said, 'I hope you are good-tempered; next door to me I do not like any one who bites.'

Just then a horse's head looked over from the stall beyond. The ears were laid back, and the eye looked rather ill-tempered. This tall chestnut mare, with a long, handsome neck, looked across to me and said, 'So it is you who have turned me out of my box. Is it not a very strange thing for a colt like you to come and turn a lady out of her own home?'

'I beg your pardon,' I said, 'I have turned no one out. The man who brought me put me here, and I had nothing to do with it. And as to my being a colt, I am turned four years old, and am a grown-up horse. I never yet had words with horse or mare, and it is my wish to live at peace.'

'Well,' she said, 'we shall see. Of course, I do not want to have words with a young thing like you.'

I said no more.

In the afternoon when she went out, Merrylegs told me all about the mare.

'The thing is this,' said Merrylegs. 'Ginger has a bad habit of biting and snapping: that is why she is called Ginger. When she was in the loose-box, she used to snap very much. One day she bit James in the arm and made it bleed, and so Miss Flora and Miss Jessie, who are very fond of me, were afraid to come into the stable. They used to bring me nice things to eat—an apple, or a carrot, or a piece of bread; but after Ginger stood in that box, they dare not come, and I miss them very much. I hope, if you do not bite or snap, that they will now come again.'

I told him I never bit anything but grass, hay, and corn, and could not think what pleasure Ginger found in it.

'Well, I don't think she does find pleasure in it,' said Merrylegs; 'it is just a bad habit. She says no one was ever kind to her, and so why should she not bite? Of course it is a very bad habit; but I am sure, if all she says be true, she must have been very ill-used before she came here. John and James do all they can to please her, and our master never uses a whip if a horse behaves himself; so I think she might be good-tempered here.

'You see,' he said with a wise look, 'I am twelve years old; I know a great deal, and I can tell you there is not a better place for a horse all round the country than this. John is the best groom that ever was; he has been here fourteen years; and you never saw such a kind boy as James is. So it is all Ginger's own fault that she did not stay in that box.'

CHAPTER FIVE

A FAIR START

THE name of the coachman was John Manly. He had a wife and one little child and they lived in the coachman's cottage very near the stables.

The next morning he took me into the yard and gave me a good grooming. Just as I was going into my box with my coat soft and bright, the Squire came in to look at me, and seemed pleased.

'John,' he said, 'I meant to have tried the new horse this morning, but I have other business. You may as well take him for a round after breakfast. Go by the common and the Highwood, and come back by the water-mill and the river; that will show his paces.'

'I will, sir,' said John.

After breakfast he came and fitted me with a bridle. He was very particular in letting out and taking in the straps, to fit my head comfortably. Then he brought the saddle, but it was not broad enough for my back; he saw this in a moment, and went for another, which fitted nicely. He rode me at first slowly, then at a trot, and afterwards at a canter; and when we were on the common he gave me a light touch with his whip, and we had a splendid gallop.

'Ho, ho! my boy,' he said, as he pulled me up, 'you would like to follow the hounds, I think.'

As we came back through the park we met the Squire and Mrs. Gordon walking. They stopped, and John jumped off.

'Well, John, how does he go?'

'First-rate, sir,' answered John. 'He is as fleet as a deer, and has a fine spirit, too; but the lightest touch of the rein will guide him. Down at the end of the common we met one of those travelling carts hung all over with baskets, rugs, and such like. You know, sir, many horses will not pass these carts quietly; but he just took a good look at it, and then went on as quietly and pleasantly as could be.

'Some men were shooting rabbits near the Highwood, and a gun went off close by; he pulled up a little and looked, but did not stir a step to right or left. I just held the rein steady and did not hurry him; it's my opinion he has not been frightened or ill-used while he was young.' ..

'That's well,' said the Squire. 'I will try him myself to-morrow.'

The next day I was brought up for my master. I remembered my mother's counsel and my good old master's, and I tried to do exactly what the Squire wanted me to do. I found he was a very good rider, and thoughtful for his horse, too. When we came home, the lady was at the hall door as he rode up.

'Well, my dear,' she said, 'how do you like him?'

'He is exactly what John said, my dear. A pleasanter creature I never wish to mount. What shall we call him?'

'Would you like Ebony?' said she; 'he is as black as ebony.'

'No; not Ebony.'

'Will you call him Blackbird, like your uncle's old horse?'

'No; he is far handsomer than old Blackbird ever was.'

'Yes,' she said, 'he is really quite a beauty, and he has such a sweet, good-tempered face and such a fine, intelligent eye—what do you say to calling him Black Beauty?'

'Black Beauty—why, yes, I think that is a very good name. If you like, it shall be so;' and that is how I got my name.

When John went into the stable, he told James that master and mistress had chosen a good sensible English name for me that meant something; not like Marengo, or Pegasus, or Abdullah. They both laughed, and James said: 'If it were not for bringing back the past, I should have named him Rob Roy, for I never saw two horses more alike.'

'That's no wonder,' said John. 'Didn't you know that Farmer Grey's old Duchess was the mother of them both?'

I had never heard that before. So poor Rob Roy who was killed at the hunt was my brother! I do not wonder that my mother was so troubled. It seems that horses have no relations; at least, they never know each other after they are sold.

John seemed very proud of me: he used to make my mane and tail almost as smooth as a lady's hair, and he would talk to me a great deal. Of course, I did not understand all he said, but I learned more and more to know what he *meant*, and what he wanted me to do. I grew very fond of him, because he was so gentle and kind, and seemed to know just how a horse feels; and when he cleaned me, he knew the tender places and the ticklish places; and when he brushed my head, he went as carefully over my eyes as if they were his own, and never stirred up any ill-temper.

James Howard, the stable boy, was just as gentle and pleasant in his way; so I thought myself well off. There was another man who helped in the yard, but he had very little to do with Ginger and me.

A few days after this I had to go in the carriage with Ginger. I wondered how we should get on together; but except laying her ears back when I was led up to her, she behaved very well. She did her work honestly, and did her full share; and I never wish to have a better partner in double harness.

When we came to a hill, instead of slackening her pace, she would throw her weight right into the collar, and pull away straight up. We had both the same sort of courage at our work; and John had more often to hold us in than to urge us forward. He never had to use the whip with either of us. Then our paces were much the same, and I found it very easy to keep step with her when trotting. This made it pleasant, and master always liked us to keep step well, and so did John. After we had been out two or three times together we grew quite friendly and sociable; this made me feel very much at home.

As for Merrylegs, he and I soon became great friends. He was such a cheerful, plucky, good-tempered little fellow that he was a favourite with every one, and especially with Miss Jessie and Miss Flora, who used to ride him about in the orchard and have fine games with him and their little dog Frisky.

Our master had two other horses that stood in another stable. One was Justice, a roan cob, used for riding, or for the luggage cart; the other was an old brown hunter, named Sir Oliver; he was past work now, but was a great favourite with the master, who gave him the run of the park; he sometimes did a little light carting on the estate, or carried one of the young ladies when they rode out with their father; for he was very gentle, and could be trusted with a child as well as Merrylegs. The cob was a strong, well-made, good-tempered horse, and we sometimes had a little chat in the paddock, but of course I could not be so intimate with him as with Ginger, who stood in the same stable.

CHAPTER SIX

LIBERTY

I was quite happy in my new place, and if there was one thing that I missed, it must not be thought I was discontented. All who had to do with me were good, and I had a light, airy stable, and the best of food.

What more could I want? Why, liberty! For three years and

a half of my life I had had all the liberty I could wish for; but now, week after week, month after month, and no doubt year after year, I must stand up in a stable night and day except when I am wanted; and then I must be just as steady and quiet as any old horse who has worked twenty years. I must wear straps here and straps there, a bit in my mouth, and blinkers over my eyes.

Now, I am not complaining, for I know it must be so. I mean only to say that for a young horse, full of strength and spirits, who has been used to some large field or plain where he can fling up his head, toss up his tail, gallop away at full speed, and then go round and back again with a snort to his companions —I say that it is hard never now to have a bit more liberty to do as he likes.

Sometimes when I have had less exercise than usual, I have felt so full of life and spring that when John has taken me out to exercise I really could not keep quiet. Do what I would, it seemed as if I must jump, dance, or prance; and many a good shake I know I must have given him, especially at the first, but he was always good and patient.

'Steady, steady, my boy,' he would say; 'wait a while, and we'll have a good swing, and soon get the tickle out of your feet.' Then, as soon as we were out of the village, he would give me a few miles at a spanking trot, and bring me back as fresh as before, only clear of the fidgets, as he called them.

Spirited horses, when not enough exercised, are often called skittish, when in fact it is only play; and some grooms will punish them, but our John did not; he knew it was only high spirits. Still, he had his own ways of making me understand by the tone of his voice or the touch of the rein. If he was very serious and quite determined, I always knew it by his voice, and that had more power over me than anything else, for I was very fond of him.

I ought to say that sometimes we had our liberty for a few hours; this used to be on fine Sundays in the summer-time. The carriage never went out on Sundays, because the church was not far off.

It was a great treat to us to be turned out into the home

paddock or the old orchard: the grass was so cool and soft to
our feet; the air was so sweet, and the freedom to do as we
liked—to gallop, lie down, roll over on our backs, or nibble the
sweet grass—was so pleasant. Then, as we stood together under
the shade of the large chestnut tree, was a very good time for
talking.

CHAPTER SEVEN

GINGER

ONE day, when Ginger and I were standing alone in the shade,
we had a long talk. She wanted to know all about my bringing
up and breaking in; so I told her.

'Well,' she said, 'if I had had your bringing up I might have
as good a temper as you; but now I don't believe I ever shall.'

'Why not?' I said.

'Because it has been all so different with me,' she replied. 'I
never had anyone, horse or man, that was kind to me, or that
I cared to please; for in the first place I was taken from my
mother as soon as I was weaned, and put with a lot of other
young colts; none of them cared for me, and I cared for none of
them. There was no kind master like yours to look after me,
talk to me, and bring me nice things to eat.

'The man that had the care of us never gave me a kind word
in my life. I do not mean that he ill-used me, but he did not
care for us more than to see that we had plenty to eat and were
sheltered in the winter.

'A footpath ran through our field, and very often the big
boys passing through would fling stones to make us gallop. I
was never hit, but one fine young colt was badly cut in the face,
and I should think it would leave a scar for life. We did not
mind the boys, but of course it made us more wild, and we
settled it in our minds that boys were our enemies. We had
very good fun in the meadows, either galloping up and down
and chasing each other round and round the field, or standing
still under the shade of the trees.

'But when it came to breaking in, that was a bad time for me. Several men came to catch me, and when at last they closed me in at one corner of the field, one caught me by the forelock, another took me by the nose, holding it so tight I could hardly draw my breath, and a third, grasping my underjaw in his hard hand, wrenched my mouth open; and so by force they got on the halter and put the bar into my mouth.

'Then one dragged me along by the halter, and another flogged me behind. This was the first experience I had of man's kindness: it was all force. They did not give me a chance to know what they wanted. I was high bred, with a great deal of spirit and, no doubt, was very wild and gave them plenty of trouble; but then it was dreadful to be shut up in a stall, day after day, instead of having my liberty. I fretted and pined and wanted to get loose. You know yourself, it's bad enough when you have a kind master and plenty of coaxing; but there was nothing of that sort for me.

'There was one—the old master, Mr. Ryder—who, I think, could soon have brought me round, and have done anything with me; but he had given up all the hard part of the trade to his son and to another experienced man. My master came only at times to oversee.

'His son was a strong, tall, bold man called Samson; and he used to boast that he had never found a horse that could throw him. There was no gentleness in him as there was in his father, but only hardness: a hard voice, a hard eye, and a hard hand. I felt from the first that what he wanted was to wear all the spirit out of me, and just make me into a quiet, humble, obedient piece of horse-flesh. "Horse-flesh!" Yes, that is all that he thought about;' and Ginger stamped her foot as if the very thought of him made her angry.

Then she went on: 'If I did not do exactly what he wanted he would get put out, and make me run round with that long rein in the training field till he had tired me out. I think he drank a good deal, and I am quite sure that the oftener he drank the worse it was for me.

'One day he had worked me hard in every way he could, and when I lay down I was tired, miserable, and angry; it all seemed so hard. The next morning, he came for me early, and ran me round again for a long time. I had scarcely had an hour's rest when he came again for me with a saddle and bridle and a new kind of bit.

'I could never quite tell how it came about. He had only just mounted me on the training ground, when something I did put him out of temper, and he jerked me hard with the rein. The new bit was very painful, and I reared up suddenly; this angered him still more, and he began to flog me.

'I felt my whole spirit set against him, and I began to kick, and plunge, and rear as I had never done before; we had a regular fight. For a long time he stuck to the saddle and punished me cruelly with his whip and spurs; but my blood was thoroughly up, and I cared for nothing he could do if only I could get him off.

'At last, after a terrible struggle, I threw him off backwards. I heard him fall heavily upon the turf, and, without looking behind me, galloped off to the other end of the field; there I turned round and saw my persecutor slowly rise from the ground and go into the stable. I stood under an oak-tree and watched, but no one came to catch me.

'Time passed; the sun was very hot, the flies swarmed round me and settled on my bleeding flanks where the spurs had dug in. I felt hungry, for I had not eaten since the early morning; but there was not enough grass in that meadow for a goose to live on. I wanted to lie down and rest, but with the saddle strapped tightly on my back there was no comfort, nor was there a drop of water to drink. The afternoon wore on, and the sun got low. I saw the other colts led in, and knew they were having a good feed.

'At last, just as the sun went down, I saw the old master come out with a sieve in his hand. He was a very fine old gentleman with quite white hair, but I should know him by his voice amongst a thousand. It was not high, nor yet low, but full, clear, and kind; and when he gave orders it was so steady and decided that every one, both horses and men, knew that he expected to be obeyed.

'He came quietly along, now and then shaking about the

oats that he had in the sieve, speaking cheerfully and gently to me: "Come along, lassie, come along, lassie; come along, come along." I stood still and let him come up.

'He held the oats towards me and I began to eat without fear; his voice took all my fear away. He stood by, patting and stroking me while I was eating, and seeing the clots of blood on my side he seemed very vexed. "Poor lassie, it was a bad business, a bad business!" Then he quietly took the rein and led me to the stable.

'Just at the door stood Samson. I laid my ears back and snapped at him. "Stand back," said the master, "and keep out of her way; you've done a bad day's work for this filly." He growled out something about a vicious brute. "Hark ye," said his father, "a bad-tempered man will never make a good-tempered horse. You've not learned your trade yet, Samson."

'Then he led me into my box, took off the saddle and bridle with his own hands, and tied me up. Calling for a pail of warm water and a sponge, he took off his coat, and while the stable man held the pail, he sponged my sides for some time so tenderly that I was sure he knew how sore and bruised they were. "Whoa! my pretty one," he said; "stand still." His very voice did me good, and the bathing was very comforting.

'The skin was so broken at the corners of my mouth that I could not eat the hay, for the stalks hurt me. He looked closely at my mouth, shook his head, and told the man to fetch me a good bran mash and put some meal into it. How good that mash was! so soft and healing to my mouth. He stood by, stroking me and talking to the man all the time I was eating. "If a high-mettled creature like this," said he, "can't be broken in by fair means, she never will be good for anything."

'After that he often came to see me, and when my mouth was healed, the other breaker, Job, went on training me. As he was steady and thoughtful, I soon learned what he wanted.'

CHAPTER EIGHT

GINGER'S STORY CONTINUED

THE next time that Ginger and I were together in the paddock, she told me about her first place.

'After my breaking in,' she said, 'I was bought by a dealer to match another chestnut horse. For some weeks he drove us together, and then we were sold to a fashionable gentleman, and were sent up to London. I had been driven with a bearing rein by the dealer, and I hated it worse than anything else; but in this place we were reined far tighter, the coachman and his master thinking in this way we looked more stylish. We were often driven about in the Park and other fashionable places. You, who never had a bearing rein on, don't know what it is; but I can tell you it is dreadful.

'I like to toss my head about, and hold it as high as any horse; but you can fancy how it would feel if you tossed your head up high and were obliged to hold it there for hours together, not able to move it at all, except with a jerk still higher; and all this time your neck was aching till you did not know how to bear it.

'Besides this, you have two bits instead of one; and mine was a sharp one. It hurt my tongue and jaw, and the blood from my tongue coloured the froth that kept flying from my lips, as I chafed and fretted at the bits and rein. It was worse when we had to stand by the hour waiting for our mistress at some grand party or entertainment; and if I fretted or stamped with impatience, the whip was laid on. It was enough to drive one mad.'

'Did not your master take any thought for you?' I said.

'No,' said she, 'he cared only to have a stylish turn-out, as they call it. I think he knew very little about horses; he left that to his coachman, who told him that I was of an irritable temper, and that I had not been well broken to the bearing rein, but that I should soon get used to it.

'I grew more and more restless and irritable; I could not help it. Then I began to snap and kick when any one came to harness me, and for this the groom beat me. One day, as they had just buckled us into the carriage and were straining my head up with that rein, I began to plunge and kick with all my might. I soon broke a lot of harness, and kicked myself clear; so my stay there was ended.

'Soon I was sent to Tattersall's to be sold. Of course, I could not be warranted free from vice; so nothing was said about that. My handsome appearance and good paces soon brought a gentleman to bid for me, and I was bought by another dealer. He tried me in all kinds of ways and with different bits, and soon found out what I could bear. At last he drove me quite without a bearing rein, and then sold me as a perfectly quiet horse to a gentleman in the country.

'He was a good master, and I was getting on very well, but his old groom left him and a new one came. This man was as hard-tempered and hard-handed as Samson; he always spoke in a rough, impatient voice, and if I did not move in the stall the moment he wanted me, he would hit me above the hocks with the stable broom or the fork, whichever he might have in his hand. Everything he did was rough, and I began to hate him; he wanted to make me afraid of him, but I was too high-mettled for that.

'One day when he had aggravated me more than usual, I bit him; this of course put him in a great rage, and he began to hit me about the head with a riding whip. After that, he never dared to come into my stall again, either my heels or my teeth were ready for him, and he knew it. I was quite quiet with my master, but of course he listened to what the man said, and so I was sold again.

'The same dealer heard of me, and said he thought he knew of a place where I should do well. "'Twas a pity," he said, "that such a fine horse should go to the bad for want of a real good chance"; and the end of it was that I came here not long before you did. I had now made up my mind that men were my natural enemies, and that I must defend myself. Of course, it is very different here; but who knows how long it will last? I

wish I could think about things as you do; but I can't after all
I have gone through.'

'Well,' I said, 'I think it would be a real shame if you were
to bite or kick John or James.'

'I don't mean to,' she said, 'while they are good to me. I did
once bite James pretty sharp, but John said, "Try her with
kindness," and instead of punishing me as I expected, James
came to me with his arm bound up, and brought me a bran
mash and stroked me; and I have never snapped at him since;
and I won't again.'

I was sorry for Ginger, but of course I knew very little then,
and I thought most likely she made the worst of it. However, I
found that as the weeks went on she grew much more gentle
and cheerful, and lost the watchful, defiant look that she used
to turn on any strange person who came near her. And one day
James said, 'I do believe that mare is getting fond of me, she
quite whinnied after me this morning when I had been rubbing
her forehead.'

'Ay, ay, Jim, 'tis the Birtwick balls,' said John; 'she'll be as
good as Black Beauty by-and-by; kindness is all the physic she
wants, poor thing!' Master noticed the change too, and one
day when he got out of the carriage and came to speak to us, as
he often did, he stroked her beautiful neck. 'Well, my pretty
one, well, how do things go with you now? You are a good bit
happier than when you came to us, I think.'

She put her nose up to him in a friendly, trustful way, while
he rubbed it gently.

'We shall make a cure of her, John,' he said.

'Yes, sir, she's wonderfully improved; she's not the same
creature that she was. It's the Birtwick balls, sir,' said John,
laughing.

This was a little joke of John's; he used to say that a regular
course of the Birtwick horse-balls would cure almost any vicious
horse. These balls, he said, were made up of patience and
gentleness, firmness and petting: one pound of each to be mixed
with half a pint of common sense, and given to the horse every
day.

CHAPTER NINE

MERRYLEGS

MR. BLOMEFIELD, the Vicar, had a large family of boys and girls, who sometimes came to play with Miss Jessie and Miss Flora. One of the girls was as old as Miss Jessie; two of the boys were older, and there were several little ones. When they came there was plenty of work for Merrylegs, for nothing pleased them so much as getting on him in turn, and riding him all about the orchard and the home paddock by the hour together.

One afternoon he had been out with them a long time, and when James brought him in and put on his halter, he said:—

'There, you rogue, mind how you behave yourself, or we shall get into trouble.'

'What have you been doing, Merrylegs?' I asked.

'Oh!' said he, tossing his little head, 'I have only been giving these young people a lesson. They did not know when they had had enough, nor when I had had enough; so I just pitched them off backwards: that was the only thing they could understand.'

'What!' said I, 'you threw the children off? I thought you knew better than that! Did you throw Miss Jessie or Miss Flora?'

He looked very much offended, and said:—

'Of course not; I would not do such a thing for the best oats that ever came into the stable. Why I am as careful of our young ladies as the master could be; and as for the little ones, it is I who teach them to ride. When they seemed frightened or a little unsteady on my back, I go as smoothly and as quietly as old pussy when she is after a bird; and when they are all right, I go on again faster, just to use them to it. So don't you trouble yourself preaching to me; I am the best friend and riding-master those children have.

'It is not they; it is the boys. Boys,' said he, shaking his

33

mane, 'are quite different; they must be broken in, as we were broken in when we were colts, and must just be taught what's what.

'The other children had ridden me about for nearly two hours, and then the boys thought it was their turn; and so it was, and I was quite agreeable. They rode me in turn, and I galloped them about, up and down the fields and all about the orchard for a good hour.

'They had each cut a great hazel stick for a riding-whip, and laid it on a little too hard; but I took it in good part, till at last I thought we had had enough; so I stopped two or three times by way of a hint. Boys, you see, think a horse or pony is like a steam-engine or threshing-machine, that can go on as long and as fast as they please. They never think that a pony can get tired, or have any feelings; so as the one whipping me could not understand, I just rose up on my hind legs and let him slip off behind—that was all. He mounted me again, and I did the same. Then the other boy got up; and as soon as he began to use his stick, I laid him on the grass; and so on, till they were able to understand: that was all.

'They are not bad boys; they don't wish to be cruel. I like them very well; but you see I had to give them a lesson. When they brought me to James and told him, I think he was very angry to see such big sticks. He said they were only fit for drovers or gipsies, and not for young gentlemen.'

'If I had been you,' said Ginger, 'I would have given those boys a good kick, and that would have given them a lesson.'

'No doubt you would,' said Merrylegs; 'but then I am not quite such a fool (begging your pardon) as to anger our master or make James ashamed of me. Besides, those children are under my charge when they are riding; I tell you they are entrusted to me. Why, only the other day I heard our master say to Mrs. Blomefield, "My dear madam, you need not be anxious about the children; my old Merrylegs will take as much care of them as you or I could: I assure you I would not sell that pony for any money, he is so perfectly good-tempered and trustworthy." Do you think I am such an ungrateful brute as to forget all the kind treatment I have had here for five years, and all the trust they place in me, and turn vicious because a couple of ignorant boys used me badly?

'No! no! you never had a good place where they were kind to you, and so you don't know. I'm sorry for you, but I can tell you good places make good horses. I wouldn't vex our people for anything; I love them, I do,' said Merrylegs; and he gave a low 'Ho, ho, ho,' through his nose, as he used to do in the morning when he heard James's footstep at the door.

'Besides,' he went on, 'if I took to kicking, where should I be? Why, sold off in a jiffy with no character; and I might find myself slaved about under a butcher's boy; or worked to death at some seaside place where no one cared for me, except to find out how fast I could go; or flogged along in some cart with three or four great men in it going out for a Sunday spree, as I have often seen in the place I lived in before I came here. No,' said he, shaking his head, 'I hope I shall never come to that.'

CHAPTER TEN

A TALK IN THE ORCHARD

GINGER and I were not of the regular tall, carriage-horse breed; we had more of the racing blood in us. We stood about fifteen and a half hands high, and were therefore just as good for riding as for driving. Our master used to say that he disliked either horse or man that could do but one thing; and as he did not want to show off in London parks, he preferred a more active and useful kind of horse.

As for us, our greatest pleasure was when we were saddled for a riding party—the master on Ginger, the mistress on me, and the young ladies on Sir Oliver and Merrylegs. It was so cheerful to be trotting and cantering all together that it always put us in high spirits. I had the best of it, for I always carried the mistress. Her weight was little, her voice sweet, and her hand so light on the rein that I was guided almost without feeling it.

Oh! if people knew what a comfort to horses a light hand is, and how it keeps a good mouth and a good temper, they surely would not chuck, and drag, and pull at the rein as they often do. Our mouths are so tender, that where they have not been spoiled or hardened with bad or ignorant treatment, they feel the slightest movement of the driver's hand, and we know in an instant what is required of us. My mouth had never been spoiled, and I believe that was why the mistress preferred me to Ginger, although her paces were certainly quite as good. She used often to envy me, and said it was all the fault of breaking in, and the gag bit in London, that her mouth was not so perfect as mine; and then old Sir Oliver would say: 'There, there! don't vex yourself; you have the greatest honour; a mare that can carry a tall man of our master's weight, with all your spring and sprightly action, does not need to hold her head down because she does not carry the lady; we horses must take things as they come, and always be contented and willing so long as we are kindly used.'

I had often wondered how it was that Sir Oliver had such a very short tail; it really was only six or seven inches long, with a tassel of hair hanging from it; and on one of our holidays in the orchard I ventured to ask him by what accident he had lost his tail.

'Accident!' he snorted, with a fierce look, 'it was no accident! It was a cruel, shameful, cold-blooded act! When I was young I was taken to a place where these cruel things were done. I was tied up, and made fast so that I could not stir; and then they came and cut my long, beautiful tail through the flesh and through the bone, and took it away.'

'How dreadful!' I exclaimed.

'Dreadful! Ah, it was dreadful! but it was not only the pain, though that was terrible and lasted a long time; it was not only the indignity of having my best ornament taken from me, though that was bad; but it was this—how could I ever again brush the flies off my sides and off my hind legs. You who have tails just whisk the flies off without thinking about it; and you can't tell what a torment it is to have them settle upon you, and sting, and yet have nothing in the world with which to lash them off. I tell you it is a lifelong wrong, and a lifelong loss. But, thank Heaven! men don't do it now.'

'What did they do it for then?' said Ginger.

'For fashion!' said the old horse, with a stamp of his foot. 'For fashion! if you know what that means. There was not a well-bred young horse in my time that had not his tail docked in that shameful way, just as if the good God that made us did not know what we wanted and what looked best.'

'I suppose it is fashion that makes them strap our heads up with those horrid bits that I was tortured with in London,' said Ginger.

'Of course it is,' said he. 'To my mind, fashion is one of the most wicked things in the world. Now look, for instance, at the way they serve dogs, cutting off their tails to make them look plucky, and shearing up their pretty little ears to a point, to make them look sharp, forsooth.

'I had a dear friend once, a brown terrier—"Skye," they called her. She was so fond of me that she would never sleep out of my stall. She made her bed under the manger, and there she had a litter of five as pretty little puppies as need be. None were drowned, for they were a valuable kind; and how pleased she was with them! And when they got their eyes open and crawled about, it was a real pretty sight.

'But one day the man came and took them all away. I thought he might be afraid I should tread upon them: but it was not so. In the evening poor Skye brought them back again, one by one in her mouth; not the happy little things that they were, but bleeding and crying pitifully. They all had a piece of their tails cut off, and the soft flap of their pretty little ears was cut quite off. How their mother licked them, and how troubled she was, poor thing! I never forgot it. The wounds healed in time, and they forgot the pain; but the nice, soft flap, that of course was, intended to protect the delicate part of their ears from dust and injury, was gone for ever.

'Why don't they cut their own children's ears into points to make them look sharp? Why don't they cut the end off their noses to make them look plucky? One would be just as sensible

as the other. What right have they to torment and disfigure
God's creatures?'

Sir Oliver, though he was so gentle, was a fiery old fellow;
and what he said was all so new to me and so dreadful, that I
found a bitter feeling toward men that I had never had before
rise up in my mind. Of course, Ginger was much excited. With
flashing eyes and distended nostrils, she flung up her head,
declaring that men were both brutes and blockheads.

'Who talks about blockheads?' said Merrylegs, who just came
up from the old apple-tree, where he had been rubbing himself
against the low branch. 'Who talks about blockheads? I believe
that is a bad word.'

'Bad words were made for bad things,' said Ginger; and she
told him what Sir Oliver had said.

'It is all true' said Merrylegs sadly, 'and I've seen that about
the dogs over and over again where I lived first; but we won't
talk about it here. You know that master, John, and James are
always good to us; and talking against men in such a place as
this doesn't seem fair or grateful. You know there are good
masters and good grooms besides ours, though of course ours
are the best.'

This wise speech of good little Merrylegs, which we knew
was quite true, cooled us all down, specially Sir Oliver, who
was dearly fond of his master; and to turn the subject I said,
'Can any one tell me the use of blinkers?'

'No!' said Sir Oliver, shortly, 'because they are no use.'

'They are supposed,' said Justice in his calm way, 'to prevent
horses from shying and starting, and getting so frightened as
to cause accidents.'

'Then what is the reason they do not put them on riding
horses, especially on ladies' horses?' said I.

'There is no reason at all,' said he quietly, 'except the fashion.
They say that a horse would be so frightened to see the wheels
of his own cart or carriage coming behind him that he would
be sure to run away, although of course when he is ridden he
sees them all about him if the streets are crowded. I admit they
do sometimes come too close to be pleasant, but we don't run
away; we are used to it, and understand it. If we never had

blinkers put on, we should never want them; we should see what was there, and know what was what, and be much less frightened than by only seeing bits of things that we can't understand.'

Of course there may be some nervous horses which have been hurt or frightened when they were young; these may be the better for them: but as I never was nervous, I can't judge.

'I consider,' said Sir Oliver, 'that blinkers are dangerous things in the night. We horses can see much better in the dark than men can, and many an accident would never have happened if horses might have had the full use of their eyes.

'Some years ago, I remember, there was a hearse with two horses returning one dark night, and just by Farmer Sparrow's house, where the pond is close to the road the wheels went too near the edge, and the hearse was overturned into the water. Both the horses were drowned, and the driver hardly escaped. Of course, after this accident a stout white rail was put up that might easily be seen; but if those horses had not been partly blinded, they would of themselves have kept further from the edge, and no accident would have happened.

'When our master's carriage was overturned, before you came here, it was said that if the lamp on the left side had not gone out, John would have seen the great hole that the road-makers had left; and so he might. But if old Colin had not had blinkers on, he would have seen it, lamp or no lamp, for he was far too knowing an old horse to run into danger. As it was, he was very much hurt, the carriage was broken, and how John escaped nobody knew.'

'I should say,' said Ginger, curling her nostril, 'that these men who are so wise had better give orders that in future all foals should be born with their eyes set just in the middle of their foreheads, instead of on the side. Men always think they can improve upon Nature and mend what God has made.'

Things were getting rather sore again, when Merrylegs held up his knowing little face and said:—

'I'll tell you a secret—I believe John does not approve of blinkers; I heard him talking to master about it one day. The master said that if horses had been used to them, it might be dangerous in some cases to leave them off; and John said he thought it would be a good thing if all colts were broken in without blinkers, as was done in some foreign countries; so let us cheer up and have a run to the other end of the orchard. I believe the wind has blown down some apples, and we may just as well eat them as for the slugs to have them.'

Merrylegs' suggestion could not be resisted; so we broke off our long conversation and got up our spirits by munching some very sweet apples which lay scattered on the grass.

CHAPTER ELEVEN

PLAIN SPEAKING

THE longer I lived at Birtwick, the more proud and happy I felt at having such a place. Our master and mistress were respected and beloved by all who knew them; they were good and kind to everybody and everything; not only to men and women, but to horses and donkeys, to dogs and cats, and to cattle and birds. There was no oppressed or ill-used creature that had not a friend in them, and their servants took the same tone. If any of the village children were known to treat any creature cruelly, they soon heard about it from the Hall.

The Squire and Farmer Grey had worked together, as they said, for more than twenty years to get bearing reins on the cart horses done away with, and in our parts you seldom saw them: but sometimes if mistress met a heavily-laden horse, with his head strained up, she would stop the carriage and get out, and reason with the driver in her sweet, serious voice, and try to show him how foolish and cruel it was.

I don't think any man could withstand our mistress. I wish all ladies were like her.

Our master sometimes used to speak his mind very freely. I remember he was riding me toward home one morning, when he saw a powerful man driving towards us a light pony chaise, with a beautiful little bay pony with slender legs and a high-bred, sensitive head and face. Just as he came to the park gates the little thing turned towards them.

The man, without word or warning, wrenched the creature's head round with such force and suddenness that he nearly threw it on its haunches. Recovering itself, it was going on when he began to lash it furiously. The pony plunged forward, but the strong, heavy hand held the pretty creature back with force almost enough to break its jaw, whilst the whip still cut into him. It was a dreadful sight to me, for I knew what fearful pain it gave that delicate little mouth; but master gave me the word, and we were up with him in a second.

'Sawyer,' he cried in a stern voice, 'is that pony made of flesh and blood?'

'Flesh and blood and temper,' he said. 'He's too fond of his own will, and that won't suit me.'

The man spoke as if he was in a strong passion. He was a builder who had often been to the park on business.

'And do you think,' said master sternly, 'that treatment like this will make him fond of your will?'

'He had no business to make that turn; his road was straight on!' said the man roughly.

'You have often driven that pony up to my place,' said master; 'it only shows the creature's memory and intelligence. How did he know that you were not going there again? But that has little to do with it. I must say, Mr. Sawyer, that more unmanly, brutal treatment of a little pony it was never my painful lot to witness; and by giving way to such passion, you injure your own character as much, nay more than you injure your horse. And remember, we shall all have to be judged according to our works, whether they be towards man or towards beast.'

Master rode me home slowly, and I could tell by his voice how the thing had grieved him.

He was just as free in speaking to gentlemen of his own rank as to those below him; for another day, when we were out, we met a Captain Langley, a friend of our master. He was driving a splendid pair of grays in a kind of brake. After a little conversation the Captain said, 'What do you think of my new team,

Mr. Gordon? You know you are the judge of horses in these parts, and I should like your opinion.'

The master backed me a little so as to get a good view of them. 'They are an uncommonly handsome pair,' he said, 'and if they are as good as they look, I am sure you need not wish for anything better: but I see you yet hold to that pet scheme of yours for worrying your horses and lessening their power.'

'What do you mean,' said the other—'the bearing reins? Oh, ah! I know that's a hobby of yours. Well, the fact is, I like to see my horses hold their heads up.'

'So do I,' said master, 'as well as any man, but I don't like to see them *held up*; that takes all the shine out of it. Now you are a military man, Langley, and no doubt like to see your regiment look well on parade, "Heads up," and all that kind of thing. But you would not take much credit for your drill if all your men had their heads tied to a backboard!

'It might not do much harm on parade, except to worry and fatigue them, but how would it be in a bayonet charge against the enemy, when they want the free use of every muscle, and all their strength thrown forward? I would not give much for their chance of victory; and it is just the same with horses; you fret and worry their temper and decrease their power; you will not let them throw their weight against their work, and so they have to do too much with their joints and muscles, and of course it wears them up faster. You may depend upon it, horses were intended to have their heads free, as free as men's are, and if we could act a little more according to common sense, and a good deal less according to fashion, we should find many things work easier; besides, you know as well as I that if a horse makes a false step he has much less chance of recovering himself if his head and neck are fastened back.

'And now,' said the master laughing, 'I have given my hobby a good trot out, can't you make up your mind to mount him too, Captain? Your example would go a long way.'

'I believe you are right in theory,' said the other, 'and that's rather a hard hit about the soldiers; but—well, I'll think about it,' and so they parted.

CHAPTER TWELVE

STORMY DAY

ONE day, late in the autumn, my master had a long journey to go on business. I was put into the dog-cart, and John went with his master. I always liked to go in the dog-cart, it was so light and the high wheels ran along so pleasantly. There had been a great deal of rain, and now the wind was very high and blew the dry leaves across the road in a shower. We went merrily along till we came to the toll-bar and the low wooden bridge. The river banks were rather high, and the bridge, instead of rising, went across just level, so that in the middle, if the river was full, the water would be nearly up to the woodwork and planks; but as there were good substantial rails on each side people did not mind it.

The man at the gate said the river was rising fast, and he feared it would be a bad night. Many of the meadows were under water, and in one low part of the road the water was half-way up to my knees; the bottom was good, and master drove gently, so it was no matter.

When we got to the town, of course, I had a good bait; but as the master's business engaged him a long time, we did not start for home till rather late in the afternoon. The wind was then much higher, and I heard the master say to John he had never been out in such a storm; and so I thought, as we went along the skirts of a wood, where the great branches were swaying about like twigs, and the rushing sound of the wind through the trees was terrible.

'I wish we were well out of this wood,' said my master.

'Yes, sir,' said John, 'it would be rather awkward if one of these branches came down upon us.'

The words were scarcely out of his mouth, when there was a groan, a crack, and a splitting sound, and tearing, crashing down amongst the other trees, came an oak, torn up by the roots, which fell right across the road just before us. I will never say I was not frightened, for I was. I stopped still, and I believe I trembled. Of course, I did not turn round or run away; I was not brought up to do that. John jumped out and in a moment was at my head.

'That was a very near touch,' said my master. 'What's to be done now?'

'Well, sir, we can't drive over that tree nor yet get round it; there will be nothing for it but to go back to the four cross-ways, and that will be a good six miles before we get round to the wooden bridge again. It will make us late, but the horse is fresh.'

So back we went, and round by the cross roads; but by the time we got to the bridge it was very nearly dark, and we could just see that the water was over the middle of it; but as that happened sometimes when floods were out, master did not stop.

We were going along at a good pace, but the moment my feet touched the first part of the bridge, I felt sure there was something wrong. I dare not go forward, and so I made a dead stop. 'Go on, Beauty,' said my master, giving me a touch with the whip; but I dare not stir. He gave me a sharp cut; I jumped, but I dared not go forward.

'There's something wrong, sir,' said John; and he sprang out of the dog-cart and came to my head and looked all about. He tried to lead me forward. 'Come on, Beauty, what's the matter?' Of course I could not tell him, but I knew very well that the bridge was not safe.

Just then the man at the toll-gate on the other side ran out of the house, tossing a torch about like one mad.

'Hoy, hoy, hoy, halloo, stop!' he cried.

'What's the matter?' shouted my master.

'The bridge is broken in the middle and part of it is carried away; if you come on you'll be into the river.'

'Thank God!' said my master. 'You Beauty!' said John; and taking the bridle, he gently turned me round to the right-hand road by the river side. The sun had set some time, the wind seemed to have lulled off after that furious blast which tore up the tree. It grew darker and darker, and more and more still. I trotted quietly along, the wheels hardly making a sound on the soft road.

For a good while neither master nor John spoke; and then the master began to speak in a serious voice. I could not understand much of what they said, but I found they thought that if I had gone on as the master wanted me, most likely the bridge would have given way under us, and horse, chaise, master, and man would have fallen into the river; and as the current was flowing very strongly, and there was no light and no help at hand, it was more than likely we should all have been drowned. Master said God had given men reason by which they could find out things for themselves; but He had given animals knowledge which did not depend on reason, much more prompt and perfect in its way, by which they had often saved the lives of men.

John had many stories to tell of dogs and horses, and the wonderful things they had done. He thought people did not value their animals half enough, nor make friends of them as they ought to do. I am sure he makes friends of them if ever man does.

CHAPTER THIRTEEN

THE DEVIL'S TRADE MARK

ONE day, when John and I had been out on some business for our master, and were returning gently on a long straight road, at some distance we saw a boy trying to leap a pony over a gate. The pony would not take the leap, and the boy cut him with the whip, but he only turned off on one side; he whipped him again, but the pony turned off on the other side; Then the boy got off and gave him a hard thrashing, knocking him about the head; then he got up again and tried to make him leap the gate, kicking him all the time shamefully; but still the pony refused.

When we were nearly at the spot, the pony put down his head, threw up his heels, and sent the boy neatly over into a broad quickset hedge; and with the rein dangling from his head,

he set off home at a full gallop. John laughed out quite loudly.
'Serve him right!' he said.

'Oh! oh! oh!' cried the boy, as he struggled about amongst
the thorns; 'I say, come and help me out.'

'Thank ye,' said John, 'I think you are quite in the right place;
and maybe a little scratching will teach you not to leap a pony
over a gate that is too high for him;' and so with that John rode
off.

'It may be,' said he to himself, 'that young fellow is a liar as
well as cruel; we'll just go home by Farmer Bushby's, Beauty,
and then if anybody wants to know, you and I can tell 'em, ye
see.' So we turned off to the right, and soon came up to the
stack-yard within sight of the house. The farmer was hurrying
out into the road, and his wife was standing at the gate looking
very frightened.

'Have you seen my boy?' said Mr. Bushby, as we came up;
'he went out an hour ago on my black pony, and the creature
is just come back without a rider.'

'I should think, sir,' said John, 'he had better be without a
rider, unless he can be ridden properly.'

'What do you mean?' said the farmer.

'Well, sir, I saw your son whipping, kicking, and knocking
that good little pony about shamefully, because he would not
leap a gate that was too high for him. The pony behaved well,
sir, and showed no vice; but at last he just threw up his heels and
tipped the young gentleman into the thorn hedge. He wanted
me to help him out; but—I hope you will excuse me, sir—I did
not feel inclined to do so. There are no bones broken, sir;
he'll only get a few scratches. I love horses, and it roiles me to
see them badly used. It is a bad plan to aggravate an animal
till he uses his heels; the first time is not always the last.'

During this time the mother began to cry, 'Oh! my poor
Bill, I must go and meet him; he must be hurt.'

'You had better go into the house, wife,' said the farmer;
'Bill wants a lesson about this, and I must see that he gets it.
This is not the first time nor the second that he has ill-used
that pony, and I shall stop it. I am much obliged to you,
Manly. Good-evening.'

So we went on, John chuckling all the way home. He told James about it, who laughed and said, 'Serve him right. I knew that boy at school; he took great airs on himself because he was a farmer's son; he used to swagger about and bully the little boys. Of course we elder ones would not have any of that nonsense, and let him know that in the school and playground farmers' son and labourers' sons were all alike.

'I well remember one day, just before afternoon school, I found him at the large window catching flies and pulling off their wings. He did not see me, and I gave him a box on the ears that laid him sprawling on the floor. Well, angry as I was, I was almost frightened; he roared and bellowed in such a style. The boys rushed in from the playground, and the master ran in from the road to see who was being murdered.

'Of course, I said fair and square at once what I had done, and why; then I showed the master the poor flies, some crushed and some crawling about helpless, and I showed him the wings on the window-sill. I never saw him so angry before; but as Bill was still howling and whining, like the coward that he was, he did not give him any more punishment of that kind, but set him up on a stool for the rest of the afternoon, and said that he should not go out to play for that week.

'Then he talked to all the boys very seriously about cruelty, and said how hard-hearted and cowardly it was to hurt the weak and the helpless. But what stuck in my mind was this—he said that cruelty was the devil's own trade mark, and if we saw any one who took pleasure in cruelty, we might know to whom he belonged, for the devil was a murderer from the beginning and a tormentor to the end. On the other hand, where we saw people who loved their neighbours and were kind to man and beast, we might know that was God's mark; for "God is Love."'

'Your master never taught you a truer thing,' said John; 'there is no religion without love. People may talk as much as they like about their religion, but if it does not teach them to be good and kind to man and beast, it is all a sham—all a sham, James; and it won't stand when things come to be turned inside out and put down for what they are.'

CHAPTER FOURTEEN

JAMES HOWARD

ONE morning, early in December, John had just led me into my box after my daily exercise, and was strapping my cloth on. James was coming in from the corn-chamber with some oats, when the master came into the stable. He looked rather serious, and held an open letter in his hand. John fastened the door of my box, touched his cap, and waited for orders.

'Good-morning, John,' said the master; 'I want to know if you have any complaint to make of James?'

'Complaint, sir? No, sir.'

'Is he industrious at his work and respectful to you?'

'Yes, sir, always.'

'You never find he slights his work when your back is turned?'

'Never, sir.'

'That's well; but I must put another question: have you any reason to suspect that when he goes out with the horses to exercise them, or takes a message, he stops about talking to his acquaintance, or goes into houses where he has no business, leaving the horses outside?'

'No, sir, certainly not, and if anybody has been saying that about James, I don't believe it; and I don't mean to believe it unless I have it fairly proved before witnesses. It's not for me to say who has been trying to take away James's character; but I will say this, sir, that a steadier, smarter, more pleasant, honest young fellow I never had in this stable. I can trust his word and I can trust his work.

'He is gentle and clever with the horses, and I would rather have them in his charge than in that of half the young fellows I know in laced hats and liveries; and whoever wants a character of James Howard,' said John, with a decided jerk of his head, 'let them come to John Manly.'

The master stood all this time grave and attentive; but as

48

John finished his speech, a broad smile spread over his face, and looking kindly across at James, who all this time had stood still at the door, he said: 'James, my lad, set down the oats and come here. I am very glad to find that John's opinion of your character agrees so exactly with my own. John is a cautious man,' he said, with a droll smile, 'and it is not always easy to get his opinion about people; so I thought if I beat the bush on this side, the birds would fly out, and I should learn what I wanted to know quickly; so now we will come to business.

'I have a letter from my brother-in-law, Sir Clifford Williams, of Clifford Hall. He wants me to find him a trustworthy young groom, about twenty or twenty-one, who knows his business. His old coachman, who has lived with him twenty years, is getting feeble, and he wants a man to work with him and get into his ways, so that he would be able, when the old man was pensioned off, to step into his place. He would have eighteen shillings a week at first, a stable suit, a driving suit, a bedroom over the coach-house, and a boy under him. Sir Clifford is a good master, and if you could get the place, it would be a good start for you. I don't want to part with you, and if you left us I know John would lose his right hand.'

'That I should sir,' said John, 'but I would not stand in his light for the world.'

'How old are you, James?' said the master.

'Nineteen next May, sir.'

'That's young. What do you think, John?'

'Well, sir, it's young; but he is as steady as a man, strong, and well grown; and though he has not had much experience in driving, he has a light, firm hand, a quick eye, and is very careful. I am quite sure no horse of his will be ruined for want of having his feet and shoes looked after.'

'Your word will go the farthest, John,' said the master, 'for Sir Clifford adds in a postscript, "If I could find a man trained by your John, I should like him better than any other." So James, lad, think it over; talk to your mother at dinner-time and then let me know what you wish.'

In a few days after this conversation it was fully settled that

James should go to Clifford Hall in a month or six weeks, as it best suited his master, and in the meantime he was to get all the practice in driving that could be given him.

CHAPTER FIFTEEN

THE OLD OSTLER

AFTER this, my master and mistress decided to pay a visit to some friends who lived about forty-six miles from our home, and James was to drive them. The first day we travelled thirty-two miles; there were some long, heavy hills, but James drove so carefully and thoughtfully that we were not at all harassed. He never forgot to put on the drag as we went downhill, nor to take it off at the right place. He kept our feet on the smoothest part of the road; and if the uphill was very long, he set the wheels a little across the road so that the carriage should not run back, and gave us breathing time. All these little things help a horse very much, particularly if he gets kind words into the bargain.

We stopped once or twice on the road; and just as the sun was going down, we reached the town where we were to spend the night. We stopped at the principal hotel, a very large one in the Market Place. We drove under an archway into a long yard, at the farther end of which were the stables and coach-houses. Two ostlers came to take us out. The head ostler was a pleasant, active little man, with a crooked leg, and a yellow striped waistcoat. I never saw a man unbuckle harness so quickly as he did; and then with a pat and a good word he led me to a long stable with six or eight stalls in it and two or three horses. The other man brought Ginger—James stood by whilst we were rubbed down and cleaned.

I never was cleaned so lightly and quickly as by that little old man. When he had done, James stepped up and felt me over, as if he thought I could not be thoroughly done; but he found my coat as clean and smooth as silk.

'Well,' he said, 'I thought I was pretty quick, and our John quicker still, but you do beat all I ever saw for being quick and thorough at the same time.'

'Practice makes perfect,' said the crooked little ostler, 'and 'twould be a pity if it didn't. Forty years' practice, and not perfect! Ha! ha! that would be a pity. As to being quick, why, bless you! that is only a matter of habit. If you get into the habit of being quick, it is just as easy as being slow—easier, I should say. In fact, it does not agree with my health to be hulking about over a job twice as long as it need take. Bless you! I couldn't whistle if I crawled over my work as some folks do.

'You see I have been about horses ever since I was twelve years old, in hunting-stables and racing-stables. Being small, you see, I was a jockey for several years; but at the Goodwood the turf was very slippery and my poor Larkspur got a fall, and I broke my knee; and so, of course, I was of no more use there.

'But I could not live without horses, of course I couldn't, so I took to the hotels; and I can tell you it is a downright pleasure to handle an animal like this: well-bred, well-mannered, well-cared-for. Bless you! I can tell how a horse is treated. Give me the handling of a horse for twenty minutes, and I'll tell you what sort of a groom he has had.

'Look at this one, pleasant, quiet, turns about just as you want him to do, holds up his feet to be cleaned out, or anything else you please to wish. Then you'll find another fidgety, fretful, won't move the right way, or starts across the stall, tosses up his head as soon as you come near him, lays back his ears, and seems afraid of you, or else squares about at you with his heels.

'Poor things! I know what sort of treatment they have had. If they are timid, the treatment makes them start or shy; if they are high-mettled, it makes them vicious or dangerous; their tempers are mostly made when they are young. Bless you! they are like children; train 'em up in the way they should go, as the good Book says, and when they are old they will not depart from it—if they have a chance, that is.'

CHAPTER SIXTEEN

THE FIRE

Later on in the evening, a traveller's horse was brought in by the second ostler, and whilst he was cleaning him a young man with a pipe in his mouth lounged into the stable to gossip.

'I say, Towler,' said the ostler, 'just run up the ladder into the loft and bring down some hay into this horse's rack, will you? Only first lay down your pipe.'

'All right,' said the other, and went up through the trap door; and I heard him step across the floor overhead and put down the hay. James came in to look at us the last thing, and the door was locked.

I cannot say how long I had slept, nor what time in the night it was, but I woke up feeling very uncomfortable, though I hardly knew why. I got up; the air seemed all thick and choking. I heard Ginger coughing, and one of the other horses moved about restlessly. It was quite dark, and I could see nothing; but the stable was full of smoke, and I hardly knew how to breathe.

The trap door had been left open, and I thought that was the place from which the smoke came. I listened and heard a soft, rushing sort of noise, and a low crackling and snapping. I did not know what it was, but there was something in the sound so strange that it made me tremble all over. The other horses were now all awake; some were pulling at their halters, others were stamping.

At last I heard steps outside, and the ostler who had put up the traveller's horse burst into the stable with a lantern, and began to untie the horses, and try to lead them out; but he seemed in such a hurry, and was so frightened himself, that he frightened me still more. The first horse would not go with him; he tried the second and third, but they too would not stir. He came to me next and tried to drag me out of the stall by force; of course that was no use. He tried us all by turns and then left the stable.

No doubt we were very foolish, but danger seemed to be all round; there was nobody whom we knew to trust in, and all was strange and uncertain. The fresh air that had come in through the open door made it easier to breathe, but the rushing sound overhead grew louder, and as I looked upward, through the bars of my empty rack, I saw a red light flickering on the wall. Then I heard a cry of 'Fire!' outside, and the old ostler came quietly and quickly in. He got one horse out, and went to another; but the flames were playing round the trap door, and the roaring overhead was dreadful.

The next thing I heard was James's voice, quiet and cheery, as it always was.

'Come, my beauties, it is time for us to be off, so wake up and come along.' I stood nearest the door, so he came to me first, patting me as he came in.

'Come, Beauty, on with your bridle, my boy, we'll soon be out of this smother.' It was on in no time; then he took the scarf off his neck, and tied it lightly over my eyes, and, patting and coaxing, he led me out of the stable. Safe in the yard, he slipped the scarf off my eyes, and shouted, 'Here somebody! take this horse while I go back for the other.'

A tall, broad man stepped forward and took me, and James darted back into the stable. I set up a shrill whinny as I saw him go. Ginger told me afterwards that whinny was the best thing I could have done for her, for had she not heard me outside, she would never have had courage to come out.

There was much confusion in the yard; the horses were being got out of other stables, and the carriages and gigs were being pulled out of houses and sheds, lest the flames should spread farther. On the other side of the yard windows were thrown open, and people were shouting all sorts of things; but I kept my eye fixed on the stable door, where the smoke poured out thicker than ever, and I could see flashes of red light.

Presently I heard above all the stir and din a loud, clear voice, which I knew was master's:—

'James Howard! James Howard! are you there?' There was no answer, but I heard a crash of something falling in the stable, and the next moment I gave a loud, joyful neigh, for I saw

James coming through the smoke, leading Ginger with him;
she was coughing violently and he was not able to speak.

'My brave lad!' said master, laying his hand on his shoulder,
'are you hurt?'

James shook his head for he could not speak yet.

'Ay,' said the big man who held me, 'he is a brave lad, and
no mistake.'

'And now,' said master, 'when you have got your breath,
James, we'll get out of this place as quickly as we can.'

We were moving towards the entry when from the Market
Place there came a sound of galloping feet and loud rumbling
wheels.

''Tis the fire engine! the fire engine!' shouted two or three
voices. 'Stand back, make way!' and clattering and thundering
over the stones two horses dashed into the yard with the heavy
engine behind them. The firemen leaped to the ground; there
was no need to ask where the fire was—it was torching up in
a great blaze from the roof.

We got out as fast as we could into the broad, quiet Market
Place. The stars were shining, and, except for the noise behind
us, all was still. Master led the way to a large hotel on the
other side, and as soon as the ostler came, he said, 'James, I
must now hasten to your mistress; I trust the horses entirely to
you; order whatever you think is needed;' and with that he was
gone. The master did not run, but I never saw mortal man
walk so fast as he did that night.

There was a dreadful sound before we got into our stalls—
the shrieks of those poor horses that were left burning to death
in the stable were very terrible! They made both Ginger
and me feel very ill. We, however, were taken in and well
done by.

The next morning the master came to see how we were and
to speak to James. I did not hear much, for the ostler was
rubbing me down; but I could see that James looked very
happy, and I thought the master was proud of him.

Our mistress had been so much alarmed in the night that the
journey was put off till the afternoon; so James had the morning
on hand, and went first to the inn to see about our harness and

the carriage, and then to hear more about the fire. When he came back, we heard him tell the ostler about it.

At first no one could guess how the fire had been caused; but at last a man said he saw Dick Towler go into the stable with a pipe in his mouth, and when he came out he had not one and went to the tap for another. Then the under-ostler said he had asked Dick to go up the ladder to get down some hay, but told him to lay down his pipe first. Dick denied taking the pipe with him, but no one believed him.

I remember our John Manly's rule, never to allow a pipe in the stable, and thought it ought to be the rule everywhere.

James said the roof and floor had all fallen in and that only the black walls were standing. The two poor horses that could not be got out were buried under the burnt rafters and tiles.

CHAPTER SEVENTEEN

JOHN MANLY'S TALK

THE rest of our journey was very easy, and a little after sunset we reached the house of my master's friend. We were taken into a clean, snug stable where was a kind coachman, who made us very comfortable. He seemed to think a great deal of James when he heard about the fire.

'There is one thing quite clear, young man,' he said. 'Your horses know whom they can trust. It is one of the hardest things in the world to get horses out of a stable when there is either fire or flood. I don't know why they won't come out, but they won't—not one in twenty.'

We stopped two or three days at this place and then returned home. All went well on the journey; we were glad to be in our own stable again, and John was equally glad to see us.

Before James and he left us for the night, James said, 'I wonder who is coming in my place.'

'Little Joe Green at the Lodge,' said John.

'Little Joe Green! Why, he's a child!'

'He is fourteen and a half,' said John.

'But he is such a little chap!'

'Yes, he is small, but he is quick, willing, and kind-hearted too, and wishes very much to come, and his father would like it; and I know the master would like to give him the chance. He said, if I thought he would not do, he would look out for a bigger boy; but I said I was quite agreeable to try him for six weeks.'

'Six weeks!' said James, 'why, it will be six months before he can be of much use! It will make you a deal of work, John.'

'Well,' said John with a laugh, 'work and I are very good friends; I never was afraid of work yet.'

'You are a very good man,' said James; 'I wish I may ever be like you.'

'I don't often speak of myself,' said John, 'but as you are going away from us out into the world to shift for yourself, I'll just tell you how I look on these things. I was just as old as Joseph when my father and mother died of the fever, within ten days of each other, and left me and my crippled sister Nelly, alone in the world, without a relation to whom we could look for help.

'I was a farmer's boy, not earning enough to keep myself, much less both of us, and she must have gone to the workhouse but for our mistress (Nelly calls her her angel, and she has good right to do so). The mistress went and hired a room for her with old Widow Mallet, and she gave her knitting and needle-work, when she was able to do it; and when she was ill, she sent her dinners and many nice comfortable things, and was like a mother to her. Then the master took me into the stable under old Norman, the coachman that then was. I had my food at the house and my bed in the loft, and a suit of clothes and three shillings a week, so that I could help Nelly.

'Norman might have turned round and said that at his age he could not be troubled with a raw boy from the plough-tail; but he was like a father to me, and took no end of pains with me. When the old man died some years after, I stepped into his place; and now of course I have top wages, and can lay by for a rainy day or a sunny day as it may happen; and Nelly is as happy as a bird.

'So you see, James, I am not the man that should turn up his nose at a little boy, and vex a good, kind master. No! no! I shall miss you very much, James, but we shall pull through. There's nothing like doing a kindness when 'tis put in your way, and I am glad I can do it.'

'Then,' said James, 'you don't hold with that saying, "Everybody look after himself, and take care of number one"?'

'No, indeed,' said John. 'Where would Nelly and I have been if master and mistress and old Norman had only taken care of number one? Why, she in the workhouse and I hoeing turnips! Where would Black Beauty and Ginger have been if you had only thought of number one? Why, roasted to death! No, Jim, no! that is a selfish, heathenish saying, whoever may use it, and any man who thinks he has nothing to do but take care of number one, why, it's a pity but what he had been drowned like a puppy or a kitten before he got his eyes open; that's what I think,' said John, with a very decided jerk of his head.

James laughed at this; but there was a thickness in his voice when he said, 'You have been my best friend except my mother; I hope you won't forget me.'

'No, lad, no!' said John, 'and if ever I can do you a good turn I hope you won't forget me.'

The next day Joe came to the stables to learn all he could before James left. He learned to sweep the stable, to bring in the straw and hay, and began to clean the harness, and help to wash the carriage. As he was quite too short to do anything in the way of grooming Ginger and me, James taught him upon Merrylegs, for, under John, he was to have full charge of the pony. He was a nice little bright fellow, and always came whistling to his work.

Merrylegs was a good deal put out at being 'mauled about,' as he said, 'by a boy who knew nothing;' but towards the end of the second week he told me confidentially that he thought the boy would turn out well.

At last the day came when James had to leave us; cheerful as he always was, he looked quite downhearted that morning.

'You see,' he said to John, 'I am leaving a great deal behind —my mother and Betsy, you, a good master and mistress, and the horses and my old Merrylegs. At the new place there will not be a soul I shall know. If it were not that I shall get a higher place, and be able to help my mother better, I don't think I should have made up my mind to it; it is a real pinch, John.'

'Ay, James, lad, so it is, but I should not think much of you if you could not leave your home for the first time and not feel it. Cheer up! you'll make friends there, and if you get on well— as I am sure you will— it will be a fine thing for your mother, and she will be proud enough that you have got into such a good place as that.'

So John cheered him up, but every one was sorry to lose James. As for Merrylegs, he pined after him for several days, and went quite off his appetite. So when he had exercised me, John took him out several mornings with a leading rein, and trotting and galloping by my side he got up the little fellow's spirits again, and Merrylegs was soon all right.

Joe's father would often come in and give a little help, as he understood the work, and Joe took a great deal of pains to learn, and John was quite encouraged about him.

CHAPTER EIGHTEEN

GOING FOR THE DOCTOR

ONE night, a few days after James had left, I had eaten my hay and was lying down in my straw fast asleep, when I was suddenly awakened by the stable bell ringing very loudly. I heard the door of John's house opened and his feet running up to the Hall. He was back again in no time. He unlocked the stable door and came in, calling out, 'Wake up, Beauty, you must go well now, if ever you did!' and almost before I could think, he had placed the saddle on my back and the bridle on my head. He just ran round for his coat, and then took me at a quick trot up to the Hall door. The Squire stood there with a lamp in his hand.

'Now, John,' he said, 'ride for your life—that is, for your

mistress's life; there is not a moment to lose. Give this note to Doctor White. Give your horse a rest at the inn, and be back as soon as you can.'

John said, 'Yes, sir,' and was on my back in a minute. The gardener who lived at the lodge had heard the bell ring, and was ready with the gate open. Away we went through the park, through the village, and down the hill till we came to the toll-gate. John called very loudly and thumped upon the door: the man was soon out and flung open the gate.

'Now,' said John, 'do you keep the gate open for the Doctor; here's the money,' and off we went again.

There was before us a long piece of level road by the riverside. John said to me, 'Now, Beauty, do your best,' and so I did; I wanted neither whip nor spur, and for two miles I galloped as fast as I could lay my feet to the ground. I don't believe that my old grandfather, who won the race at Newmarket, could have gone faster. When we came to the bridge John pulled me up a little and patted my neck. 'Well done, Beauty! good old fellow,' he said. He would have let me go more slowly, but my spirit was up and I was off again as fast as before.

The air was frosty, the moon bright, and it was very pleasant. We went through a village, through a dark wood, then uphill, then downhill, till after an eight miles' run we came to the town. On through the streets we went and into the Market Place. All was quite still except for the clatter of my feet on the stones—everybody was asleep. The church clock struck three as we drew up at Doctor White's door.

John rang the bell twice, and then knocked at the door like thunder. A window was thrown up, and Doctor White, in his nightcap, put his head out and said, 'What do you want?'

'Mrs. Gordon is very ill, sir; master wants you to come at once; he thinks she will die if you cannot get there—here is a note.'

'Wait,' he said, 'I will come.'

He shut the window and was soon at the door.

'The worst of it is,' he said, 'that my horse has been out all day and is quite done up; my son has just been sent for and he has taken the other. What is to be done? Can I have your horse?'

'He has come at a gallop nearly all the way, sir, and I was to give him a rest here, but I think my master would not be against it if you think fit, sir.'

'All right,' he said, 'I will soon be ready.'

John stood by me and stroked my neck. I was very hot. The Doctor came out with his riding whip.

'You need not take that, sir,' said John. 'Black Beauty will go till he drops. Take care of him, sir, if you can; I should not like any harm to come to him.'

'No! no! John,' said the Doctor, 'I hope not,' and in a minute we had left John far behind.

I will not describe our way back; the Doctor was a heavier man than John, and not so good a rider; however, I did my very best. The man at the toll-gate had it open. When we came to the hill, the Doctor drew me up. 'Now, my good fellow,' he said, 'take some breath.' I was glad he did, for I was nearly spent; but that breathing helped me on, and soon we were in the park. Joe was at the lodge gate, and my master was at the Hall door, for he had heard us coming. He spoke not a word: the Doctor went into the house with him, and Joe led me to the stable.

I was glad to get home; my legs shook under me, and I could only stand and pant. I had not a dry hair on my body, the water ran down my legs, and I steamed all over—Joe used to say, like a pot on the fire. Poor Joe! he was young and small, and as yet he knew very little, and his father, who would have helped him, had been sent to the next village; but I am sure he did the very best he knew.

He rubbed my legs and my chest, but he did not put my warm cloth on me; he thought I was so hot I should not like it. Then he gave me a pailful of water to drink. It was cold, and very good, and I drank it all; then he gave me some hay and some corn, and thinking he had done right, he went away.

Soon I began to shake and tremble, and turned deadly cold; my legs, loins, and chest ached, and I felt sore all over. Oh! how I wished for my warm, thick cloth as I stood and trembled. I wished for John, but he had eight miles to walk, so I lay down in my straw and tried to go to sleep.

After a long while I heard John at the door; I gave a low moan, for I was in great pain. He was at my side in a moment, stooping down by me. I could not tell him how ill I felt; but he seemed to know it all. He covered me up with two or three warm cloths, and then ran to the house for some hot water; then he made some warm gruel, which I drank; then, I think, I went to sleep.

John seemed to be very much put out. I heard him say to himself, over and over again, 'Stupid boy! stupid boy! No cloth put on, and I dare say the water was cold too; boys are no good;' but Joe was a good boy after all.

I was now very ill; a strong inflammation had attacked my lungs, and I could not draw my breath without pain. John nursed me night and day. He would get up two or three times in the night to come to me; my master, too, often came to see me. 'My poor Beauty,' he said one day, 'my good horse, you saved your mistress's life, Beauty! Yes, you saved her life.'

I was very glad to hear that, for it seems the Doctor had said if we had been a little longer it would have been too late. John told my master he never saw a horse go so fast in his life; it seemed as if the horse knew what was the matter. Of course I did, though John thought I did not; at least, I knew as much as this, that John and I must go at the top of our speed, and that it was for the sake of the mistress.

CHAPTER NINETEEN

ONLY IGNORANCE

I DO not know how long I was ill. Mr. Bond, the horse doctor, came every day. One day he bled me, and John held a pail for the blood. I felt very faint after it, and thought I should die. I believe they all thought so too.

Ginger and Merrylegs had been moved into the other stable, so that I might be quiet, for fever made me very quick of hearing; any little noise seemed quite loud, and I could tell every one's footstep going to and from the house. I knew all that was going on. One night John had to give me a draught; Thomas Green came in to help him.

After I had taken it and John had made me as comfortable as he could, he said he should stay half an hour to see how the medicine settled. Thomas said he would stay with him, so they went and sat down on a bench that had been brought into Merrylegs' stall, and put down the lantern at their feet that I might not be disturbed with the light.

For a while both men sat silent, and then Tom Green said in a low voice:—

'I wish, John, you'd say a bit of a kind word to Joe; the boy is quite broken-hearted; he can't eat his meals, and he can't smile. He says he knows it was all his fault, though he is sure he did the best he knew; and he says, if Beauty dies, no one will ever speak to him again. It goes to my heart to hear him; I think you might give him just a word, he is not a bad boy.'

After a short pause, John said slowly: 'You must not be too hard upon me, Tom. I know he meant no harm; I never said he did. I know he is not a bad boy, but you see I am sore myself. That horse is the pride of my heart, to say nothing of his being such a favourite with the master and mistress; and to think that his life may be flung away in this manner is more than I can bear. But if you think I am hard on the boy, I will try to give him a good word to-morrow—that is, I mean, if Beauty is better.'

'Well, John, thank you! I knew you did not wish to be too hard, and I am glad you see it was only ignorance.'

John's voice almost startled me as he answered, '*Only* ignorance! only *ignorance*! how can you talk about *only* ignorance? Don't you know that ignorance is the worst thing in the world, next to wickedness?—and which does the most mischief Heaven only knows. If people can say, "Oh! I did not know, I did not mean any harm," they think it is all right. I suppose Martha Mulwash did not mean to kill that baby when she dosed it with Dalby and soothing syrups; but she did kill it, and was tried for manslaughter.'

'And serve her right too,' said Tom. 'A woman should not

undertake to nurse a tender little child without knowing what is good or what is bad for it.'

'Bill Starkey,' continued John, 'did not mean to frighten his brother into fits when he dressed up like a ghost, and ran after him in the moonlight; but he did; and that bright, handsome little fellow, that might have been the pride of any mother's heart, is just no better than an idiot, and never will be, if he lives to be eighty years old.

'You were a good deal cut up yourself, Tom, two weeks ago, when those young ladies left your hot-house door open, with a frosty east wind blowing right in; you said it killed a good many of your plants.'

'A good many!' said Tom. 'There was not one of the tender cuttings that was not nipped off. I shall have to strike all over again, and the worst of it is, that I don't know where to go to get fresh ones. I was nearly mad when I came in and saw what was done.'

'And yet,' said John, 'I am sure the young ladies did not mean it; it was only ignorance!'

I heard no more of this conversation, for the medicine took effect and sent me to sleep, and in the morning I felt much better; but I often thought of John's words when I came to know more of the world.

CHAPTER TWENTY

JOE GREEN

JOE GREEN went on very well; he learned quickly, and was so attentive and careful that John began to trust him in many things; but, as I have said, he was small for his age, and it was seldom that he was allowed to exercise either Ginger or me. But it so happened one morning that John was out with Justice in the luggage-cart, and the master wanted a note to be taken immediately to a gentleman's house about three miles distant, and sent his orders for Joe to saddle me and take it, adding the caution that he was to ride carefully.

The note was delivered, and we were quietly returning till we came to the brickfield. Here we saw a cart heavily laden with bricks. The wheels had stuck fast in the stiff mud of some deep ruts; and the carter was shouting and flogging the two horses unmercifully. Joe pulled up. It was a sad sight. There were the two horses straining and struggling with all their might to drag the cart out, but they could not move it; the sweat streamed from their legs and flanks, their sides heaved, and every muscle was strained, whilst the man, fiercely pulling at the head of the fore-horse, swore and lashed most brutally.

'Hold hard,' said Joe, 'don't go on flogging the horses like that; the wheels are so stuck that they cannot move the cart.' The man took no heed, but went on lashing.

'Stop! pray stop,' said Joe; 'I'll help you to lighten the cart, they can't move it now.'

'Mind your own business, you impudent young rascal, and I'll mind mine.' The man was in a towering passion and the worse for drink; and so he laid on the whip again. Joe turned my head, and the next moment we were going at a round gallop towards the house of the master brickmaker. I cannot say if John would have approved of our pace, but Joe and I were both of one mind, and so angry that we could not go slower.

The house stood close by the roadside. Joe knocked at the door and shouted, 'Hallo! is Mr. Clay at home?' The door was opened, and Mr. Clay himself came out.

'Hallo, young man! you seem in a hurry; any orders from the Squire this morning?'

'No, Mr. Clay; but there's a fellow in your brickyard flogging two horses to death. I told him to stop and he wouldn't. I said I'd help him to lighten the cart, and he wouldn't; so I have come to tell you. Pray, sir, go.' Joe's voice shook with excitement.

'Thank ye, my lad,' said the man, running in for his hat. Then, pausing for a moment—'Will you give evidence of what you saw if I should bring the fellow up before a magistrate?' he asked.

'That I will,' said Joe, 'and glad to.' The man was gone, and we were on our way home at a smart trot.

'Why, what's the matter with you, Joe? you look angry all over,' said John, as the boy flung himself from the saddle.

'I am angry all over, I can tell you,' said the boy, and then in hurried, excited words, he told all that had happened. Joe was usually such a quiet, gentle, little fellow that it was wonderful to see him so roused.

'Right, Joe! you did right, my boy, whether the fellow gets a summons or not. Many folks would have ridden by and said 'twas not their business to interfere. Now, I say, that with cruelty and oppression it is everybody's business to interfere when they see it; you did right, my boy.'

Joe was quite calm by this time, and proud that John had approved of him. He cleaned out my feet, and rubbed me down with a firmer hand than usual.

They were just going home to dinner when the footman came down to the stable to say that Joe was wanted directly in master's private room; there was a man brought up for ill-using horses, and Joe's evidence was wanted. The boy flushed up to his forehead, and his eyes sparkled. 'They shall have it,' said he.

'Put yourself a bit straight,' said John. Joe gave a pull at his necktie and a twitch at his jacket, and was off in a moment. Our master being one of the country magistrates, cases were often brought to him to settle, or say what should be done.

In the stable we heard no more for some time, as it was the men's dinner-hour. But when Joe came next into the stable I saw he was in high spirits; he gave me a good-natured slap and said, 'We won't see such things done, will we, old fellow?' We heard afterwards that he had given his evidence so clearly, and the horses were in such an exhausted state, bearing marks of such brutal usage, that the carter was committed to take his trial, and might possibly be sentenced to two or three months in prison.

It was wonderful what a change had come over Joe. John laughed, and said he had grown an inch taller in that week; and I believe he had. He was just as kind and gentle as before, but there was more purpose and determination in all that he did—as if he had jumped at once from a boy into a man.

CHAPTER TWENTY-ONE

THE PARTING

I HAD now lived in this happy place three years, but sad changes
were about to come over us. We heard from time to time that
our mistress was ill. The Doctor was often at the house, and
the master looked grave and anxious. Then we heard that she
must leave her home at once and go to a warm country for two
or three years. The news fell upon the household like the
tolling of a death-bell. Everybody was sorry; but the master
began directly to make arrangements for breaking up his
establishment and leaving England. We used to hear it talked
about in our stable; indeed, nothing else was talked about.

John went about his work silent and sad, and Joe scarcely
whistled. There was a great deal of coming and going; Ginger
and I had full work.

The first to go were Miss Jessie and Miss Flora with their
governess. They came to bid us good-bye. They hugged poor
Merrylegs like an old friend, and so indeed he was. Then we
heard what had been arranged for us. Master had sold Ginger
and me to his old friend the Earl of W——, for he thought we
should have a good place there. Merrylegs he had given to the
Vicar, who was wanting a pony for Mrs. Blomefield; but it was
on the condition that he should never be sold, and that when
he was past work he should be shot and buried.

Joe was engaged to take care of him, and to help in the
house; so I thought that Merrylegs was well off. John had the
offer of several good places, but he said he should wait a little
and look round.

The evening before they left, the master came into the stable
to give some directions and to give his horses the last pat. He
seemed very low-spirited; I knew that by his voice. I believe
we horses can tell more by the voice than many men can.

'Have you decided what to do, John?' he said. 'I find you
have not accepted any of those offers.'

'No, sir, I have made up my mind that if I could get a situation with some first-rate colt-breaker and horse-trainer, it would be the right thing for me. Many young animals are frightened and spoiled by wrong treatment, which need not be if the right man took them in hand. I always get on well with horses, and if I could help some of them to a fair start, I should feel as if I was doing some good. What do you think of it, sir?'

'I don't know a man anywhere,' said master, 'that I should think so suitable for it as yourself. You understand horses, and somehow they understand you, and in time you might set up for yourself; I think you could not do better. If in any way I can help you, write to me; I shall speak to my agent in London, and leave your character with him.'

He asked John about his future, and then thanked him for his long and faithful service; but that was too much for John. 'Pray don't, sir, I can't bear it. You and my dear mistress have done so much for me that I could never repay it; but we shall never forget you sir, and please God we may some day see mistress back again like herself; we must keep up hope, sir.' Master gave John his hand, but he did not speak; and they both left the stable.

The last sad day had come; the footman and the heavy luggage had gone off the day before, and there was only master and mistress and her maid left. Ginger and I brought the carriage up to the hall door for the last time. The servants brought out cushions and rugs and many other things; and when all were arranged, master came down the steps carrying the mistress in his arms (I was on the side next the house and could see all that went on). He placed her carefully in the carriage, while the house servants stood round crying.

'Good-bye again,' he said as he got in; 'we shall not forget any of you—drive on, John.'

Joe jumped up, and we trotted slowly through the park and through the village, where the people were standing at their doors to have a last look and to say, 'God bless them!'

When we reached the railway station, I think mistress walked from the carriage to the waiting-room. I heard her say in her own sweet voice, 'Good-bye, John; God bless you.' I felt the rein twitch, but John made no answer, perhaps he could not speak. As soon as Joe had taken the things out of the carriage, John called him to stand by the horses while he went on the platform. Poor Joe! he stood close up to our heads to hide his tears.

Very soon the train came puffing up into the station. Two or three minutes after the doors were slammed to, the guard whistled, and the train glided away, leaving behind it only clouds of white steam and some very heavy hearts.

When it was quite out of sight, John came back.

'We shall never see her again,' he said—'never.' He took the reins, mounted the box, and drove slowly home with Joe; but it was not our home now.

CHAPTER TWENTY-TWO

EARLSHALL

THE next morning after breakfast Joe put Merrylegs into the mistress's low chaise to take him to the vicarage. He came first and said good-bye to us, and Merrylegs neighed to us from the yard. Then John put the saddle on Ginger and the leading rein on me, and rode us across the country about fifteen miles to Earlshall Park, where the Earl of W—— lived. Here was a very fine house and a great deal of stabling.

We went into the yard through a stone gateway, and John asked for Mr. York. It was some time before he came. He was a fine-looking, middle-aged man, and his voice said at once that he expected to be obeyed. He was very friendly and polite to John; and after giving us a slight look, he called a groom to take us to our boxes, and invited John to take some refreshment.

We were taken to a light, airy stable and placed in boxes adjoining each other, where we were rubbed down and fed. In about half an hour John and Mr. York, who was to be our new coachman, came in to see us.

'Now, Mr. Manly,' he said, after carefully looking at us both, 'I can see no fault in these horses; but we all know that horses as well as men have their peculiarities, and that sometimes they need different treatment. I should like to know if there is anything particular in either of these that you would like to mention.'

'Well,' said John, 'I don't believe there is a better pair of horses in the country, and right grieved I am to part with them, but they are not alike. The black one is the most perfect temper I ever knew; I suppose he has never known a hard word or a blow since he was foaled, and all his pleasure seems to be what you wish to do.

'But the chestnut I fancy must have had bad treatment; we heard as much from the dealer. She came to us snappish and suspicious, but when she found what sort of place ours was, it all went off by degrees. For three years I have never seen the smallest sign of temper, and if she is well treated there is not a better or more willing animal than she is; but she is naturally of a more irritable constitution than the black horse—flies tease her more; anything wrong in the harness frets her more; and if she were ill-used or unfairly treated, she would not be unlikely to give tit for tat. You know that many high-mettled horses will do so.'

'Of course,' said York, 'I quite understand; but you know it is not easy in stables like these to have all the grooms just what they should be; I do my best, and there I must leave it. I'll remember what you have said about the mare.'

They were going out of the stable, when John stopped and said: 'I had better mention that we have never used the bearing rein with either of them; the black horse never had one on, and the dealer said it was the gag-bit that spoiled the other's temper.'

'Well,' said York, 'if they come here, they must wear the bearing rein. I prefer a loose rein myself, and his lordship is always very reasonable about horses; but my lady—that's another matter. She will have style; and if her carriage horses were not reined up right, she wouldn't look at them. I always stand out against the gag-bit, and shall do so, but the rein must be tight up when my lady rides!'

'I am sorry for it, very sorry,' said John; 'but I must go now, or I shall lose the train.'

He came round to each of us to pat and speak to us for the last time; his voice sounded very sad.

I held my face close to him, as that was all I could do to say good-bye; and then he was gone, and I have never seen him since.

The next day Lord W—— came to look at us; he seemed pleased with our appearance.

'I have great confidence in these horses,' he said, 'from the character my friend Mr. Gordon has given me of them. Of course they are not a match in colour, but my idea is that they will do very well for the carriage whilst we are in the country. Before we go to London I must try to match Baron; the black horse, I believe, is perfect for riding.'

York then told him what John had said about us.

'Well,' said he, 'you must keep an eye to the mare, and put the bearing rein easy; I dare say they will do very well with a little humouring at first. I'll mention it to her ladyship.'

In the afternoon we were harnessed and put in the carriage, and as the stable clock struck three we were led round to the front of the house. It was all very grand, and the house three or four times as large as the old one at Birtwick, but not half so pleasant, if a horse may have an opinion. Two footmen, dressed in drab livery, with scarlet breeches and white stockings, were standing ready.

Presently we heard the rustling sound of silk as my lady came down the flight of stone steps. She stepped round to look at us. She was a tall, proud-looking woman, and did not seem pleased about something; but she said nothing, and got into the carriage. This was my first time of wearing a bearing rein, and I must say, though it certainly was a nuisance not to be able to get my head down now and then, it did not pull my head higher than I was accustomed to carry it. I felt anxious about Ginger, but she seemed to be quiet and content.

The next day at three o'clock we were again at the door, and the footmen were there as before. We heard the silk dress rustle as the lady came down the steps, and in an imperious voice she said: 'York, you must put those horses' heads higher; they are not fit to be seen.'

York got down and said very respectfully: 'I beg your pardon, my lady, but these horses have not been reined up for three years, and my lord said it would be safer to bring them to it by degrees; but if your ladyship pleases, I can take them up a little more.'

'Do so,' she said.

York came round to our heads and shortened the rein one hole, I think; every little makes a difference, be it for better or worse, and that day we had a steep hill to go up. Then I began to understand what I had heard. Of course I wanted to push my head forward and take the carriage up with a will, as we had been used to do; but no, I had now to pull with my head up, and that took all the spirit out of me, and brought the strain on my back and legs.

When she came in, Ginger said: 'Now you see what it is like; but this is not bad, and if it does not get much worse than this, I shall say nothing about it, for we are very well treated here. But if they strain me up tight, why, let 'em look out! I can't bear it and I won't.'

Day by day, hole by hole, our bearing reins were shortened, and instead of looking forward with pleasure to having my harness put on as I used to do, I began to dread it. Ginger, too, seemed restless, though she said very little. At last I thought the worst was over; for several days there had been no more shortening, and I determined to make the best of it and to do my duty, though now going out was a constant harass instead of a pleasure; but the worst was not come.

CHAPTER TWENTY-THREE

A STRIKE FOR LIBERTY

ONE day my lady came down later than usual, and the silk rustled more than ever.

'Drive to the Duchess of B——'s,' she said. Then after a pause, she added: 'Are you never going to get those horses' heads up, York? Raise them at once, and let us have no more of this humouring nonsense.'

York came to me first, whilst the groom stood at Ginger's head. He drew my head back and fixed the rein so tight that it was almost intolerable, then he went to Ginger, who was impatiently jerking her head up and down against the bit, as was her way now. She had a good idea of what was coming, and the moment York took the rein off the terret in order to shorten it she took her opportunity and reared up so suddenly that York had his nose roughly hit and his hat knocked off, and the groom was nearly thrown off his legs.

At once they both flew to her head, but she was a match for them, and went on plunging, rearing, and kicking in a most desperate manner. At last she kicked right over the carriage pole and fell down, after giving me a severe blow on my near quarter.

There is no knowing what further mischief she may have done had not York promptly sat himself down flat on her head to prevent her struggling, at the same time calling out, 'Unbuckle the black horse! Run for the winch and unscrew the carriage pole; and somebody cut the trace if you can't unhitch it.'

One of the footmen ran for the winch, and another brought a knife from the house. The groom set me free from Ginger and the carriage, and led me to my box. He just turned me in as I was, and ran back to York.

I was much excited by what had happened, and if I had ever been used to kick or rear, I am sure I should have done it then; but I never had, so there I stood, angry, sore in my leg, my head still strained up to the terret on the saddle, and with no power to get it down. I was very miserable, and felt much inclined to kick the first person who came near me.

Before long, however, Ginger was led in by two grooms, a good deal knocked about and bruised. York came with her and gave his orders, and then came to look at me. In a moment he let down my head.

'Confound these bearing reins!' he said to himself. 'I thought we should have some mischief soon—master will be sorely vexed; but there—if a woman's husband can't rule her, of course a servant can't; so I wash my hands of it, and if she can't get to the Duchess's garden party, I can't help it.'

York did not say this before the men; he always spoke respectfully when they were by. Now he felt me all over and soon found the place above my hock where I had been kicked. It was swollen and painful; so he ordered it to be sponged with hot water and then some lotion to be rubbed in.

Lord W—— was much put out when he learned what had happened. He blamed York for giving way to his mistress, to which York replied that in future he would much prefer to receive his orders only from his lordship. But I think nothing came of it, for things went on the same as before. I thought York might have stood up better for his horses; but perhaps I am no judge.

Ginger was never put into the carriage again, but when her bruises were healed, one of Lord W——'s younger sons said he should like to have her; he was sure she would make a good hunter. As for me, I was obliged still to go in the carriage, and had a fresh partner, called Max, who had always been used to the tight rein. I asked him how it was he bore it.

'Well,' he said, 'I bear it because I must, but it is shortening my life, and it will shorten yours too if you have to stick to it.'

'Do you think,' I said, 'that our masters know how bad it is for us?'

'I can't say,' he replied, 'but the dealers and the horse doctors know it very well. I was at a dealer's once, who was training me and another horse to go as a pair; he was getting our heads up, as he said, a little higher and a little higher every day. A gentleman who was there asked him why he did so; "Because," said he, "people won't buy them unless we do. The London people always want their horses to carry their heads high, and to step high; of course it is very bad for the horses, but then it is good for trade. The horses soon wear up, or get diseased, and they come for another pair." That,' said Max, 'is what he said in my hearing, and you can judge for yourself.'

What I suffered for four long months with that rein it would be hard to describe; but I am quite sure that, had it lasted much longer, either my health or my temper would have given way. Before that, I never knew what it was to foam at the mouth; but now the action of the sharp bit on my tongue and jaw and the constrained position of my head and throat, always caused me to froth more or less at the mouth.

Some people think it very fine to see this, and say, 'What fine, spirited creatures!' But it is just as unnatural for horses as for men to foam at the mouth: it is a sure sign of some discomfort and should be attended to. Besides this, there was a pressure on my windpipe, which often made my breathing very uncomfortable. When I returned from my work, my neck and chest were strained and painful, my mouth and tongue tender, and I felt worn and depressed.

In my old home I always knew that John and my master were my friends; but here, although in many ways I was well treated, I had no friend. York might have known, and very likely did know, how that rein harassed me; but I suppose he took it as a matter of course that could not be helped; at any rate, nothing was done to relieve me.

CHAPTER TWENTY-FOUR

LADY ANNE, OR A RUNAWAY HORSE

EARLY in the spring Lord W—— and part of his family went up to London and took York with them. Ginger and I and some other horses were left at home for use, and the head groom was left in charge.

The Lady Harriet, who remained at the Hall, was a great invalid, and never went out in the carriage, and the Lady Anne preferred riding on horseback, with her brother or cousins. She was a perfect horsewoman, and as gay and gentle as she was beautiful. She chose me for her horse, and named me Black Auster. I enjoyed very much these rides in the clear, cold air, sometimes with Ginger, sometimes with Lizzie. This

Lizzie was a bright bay mare, almost thoroughbred, and a great favourite with the gentlemen on account of her fine action and lively spirit; but Ginger, who knew more of her than I did, told me she was rather nervous.

There was a gentleman of the name of Blantyre staying at the Hall; he always rode Lizzie, and praised her so much that one day Lady Anne ordered the side-saddle to be put on Lizzie and the other saddle on me. When we came to the door, the gentleman seemed very uneasy.

'How is this?' he said; 'are you tired of your good Black Auster?'

'Oh, no, not at all,' she replied, 'but I am amiable enough to let you ride him for once, and I will try your charming Lizzie. You must confess that in size and appearance she is far more like a lady's horse than my own favourite.'

'Do let me advise you not to mount her,' he said; 'she is a charming creature, but she is too nervous for a lady. I assure you she is not perfectly safe; let me beg you to have the saddles changed.'

'My dear cousin,' said Lady Anne, laughing, 'pray do not trouble your good, careful head about me. I have been a horsewoman ever since I was a baby, and I have followed the hounds a great many times, though I know you do not approve of ladies hunting; but still, that is the fact, and I intend to try this Lizzie that you gentlemen are all so fond of; so please help me to mount like the good friend you are.'

There was no more to be said. He placed her carefully on the saddle, looked to the bit and curb, gave the reins gently into her hand, and then mounted me. Just as we were moving off, a footman came out with a slip of paper and message from the Lady Harriet—'Would Mr. Blantyre ask this question for her at Dr. Ashley's, and bring the answer?'

The village was about a mile off, and the Doctor's house was the last in it. We went along gaily enough till we came to his gate. There was a short drive up to the house between tall evergreens. Blantyre alighted at the gate and was going to open it for Lady Anne, but she said, 'I will wait for you here; you can hang Auster's rein on the gate.'

He looked at her doubtfully—'I will not be five minutes,' he said.

'Oh, do not hurry yourself; Lizzie and I shall not run away from you.'

He hung my rein on one of the iron spikes, and was soon hidden amongst the trees. By the side of the road, a few paces off, Lizzie was standing quietly with her back to me. My young mistress was sitting easily with a loose rein, humming a little song. I listened to my rider's footsteps until they reached the house, and heard him knock at the door.

There was a meadow on the opposite side of the road, the gate of which stood open. Just then some cart horses and several young colts came trotting out in a very disorderly manner, whilst a boy behind was cracking a great whip. The colts were wild and frolicsome, and one of them bolted across the road and blundered up against Lizzie's hind legs. Whether it was the stupid colt, or the loud cracking of the whip, or both together, I cannot say; but she gave a violent kick and dashed off into a headlong gallop. It was so sudden, that Lady Anne was nearly unseated, but she soon recovered herself.

I gave a loud shrill neigh for help. Again and again I neighed, pawing the ground impatiently, and tossing my head to get the rein loose. I had not long to wait. Blantyre came running to the gate. He looked anxiously about, and just caught sight of the flying figure, now far away on the road. In an instant he sprang into the saddle. I needed no whip or spur, for I was as eager as my rider. He saw it, and giving me a free rein, and leaning a little forward, we dashed after them.

For about a mile and a half the road ran straight, then bent to the right, after which it divided into two roads. Long before we came to the bend Lady Anne was out of sight. Which way had she turned? A woman was standing at her garden gate, shading her eyes with her hand and looking eagerly up the road. Scarcely drawing the rein, Blantyre shouted, 'Which way?' 'To the right,' cried the woman, pointing with her hand, and away we went up the right-hand road; then for a moment we caught sight of her; another bend and she was hidden again. Several times we caught glimpses, and then lost them. We scarcely seemed to gain ground upon them at all.

An old road-mender was standing near a heap of stones, with shovel dropped and hands raised. As we came near he made a sign to speak. Blantyre drew the rein a little. 'To the common, to the common, sir; she has turned off there.' I knew this common very well. It was for the most part very uneven ground, covered with heather and dark green furze bushes, with here and there a scrubby old thorn-tree. There were also open spaces of fine, short grass, with ant-hills and mole-turns everywhere—the worst place I ever knew for a headlong gallop.

We had hardly turned on the common, when we caught sight again of the green habit flying on before us. My lady's hat was gone, and her long brown hair was streaming behind her. Her head and body were thrown back, as if she were pulling with all her remaining strength, and as if that strength were nearly exhausted. It was clear that the roughness of the ground had very much lessened Lizzie's speed, and there seemed a chance that we might overtake her.

Whilst we were on the high road, Blantyre had given me my head; but now with a light hand and a practised eye, he guided me over the ground in such a masterly manner, that my pace was scarcely slackened, and we were decidedly gaining on them.

About half-way across the heath there had been a wide dyke recently cut, and the earth from the cutting was cast up roughly on the other side. Surely this would stop them! But no; with scarcely a pause Lizzie took the leap, stumbled among the rough clods, and fell. Blantyre groaned, 'Now, Auster, do your best!' He gave me a steady rein, I gathered myself well together, and with one determined leap cleared both dyke and bank.

Motionless among the heather, with her face to the earth, lay my poor young mistress. Blantyre kneeled down and called her name—there was no sound.

Gently he turned her face upward; it was ghastly white, and the eyes were closed. 'Annie, dear Annie, do speak!' but there was no answer. He unbuttoned her habit, loosened her collar, felt her hands and wrists, then started up and looked wildly round for help.

At no great distance were two men cutting turf, who, seeing Lizzie running wild without a rider, had left their work to catch her.

Blantyre's 'Halloo!' soon brought them to the spot. The foremost man seemed much troubled at the sight, and asked what he could do.

'Can you ride?'

'Well, sir, I bean't much of a horseman, but I'd risk my neck for the Lady Anne; she was uncommon good to my wife in the winter.'

'Then mount this horse, my friend; your neck will be quite safe. Ride to the Doctor's and ask him to come instantly; then go on to the Hall; tell them all that you know, and bid them send me the carriage with Lady Anne's maid and other assistance. I shall stay here.'

'All right, sir, I'll do my best, and I pray God the dear young lady may open her eyes soon.' Then seeing the other man, he called out: 'Here Joe, run for some water, and tell my missis to come as quickly as she can to the Lady Anne.'

He then somehow scrambled into the saddle, and with a 'Gee up!' and a clap on my sides with both his legs, he started on his journey, making a little circuit to avoid the dyke. He had no whip, which seemed to trouble him, but my pace soon cured that difficulty, and he found the best thing he could do was to stick to the saddle, and hold me in, which he did manfully. I shook him as little as I could help, but once or twice on the rough ground he called out, 'Steady! Whoa! Steady.' On the high road we were all right; and at the Doctor's and at the Hall he did his errand like a good man and true. They asked him in to take a drop of something. 'No, no!' he said; 'I'll be back to 'em again by a short cut through the fields, and be there before the carriage.'

There was a great deal of hurry and excitement after the news became known. I was just turned into my box, the saddle and bridle were taken off, and a cloth thrown over me.

Ginger was saddled and sent off in great haste for Lord George, and I soon heard the carriage roll out of the yard.

It seemed a long time before Ginger came back and before we were left alone; and then she told me all that she had seen. 'I can't tell much,' she said; 'we went galloping nearly all the way, and got there just as the Doctor rode up. There was a woman sitting on the ground with the lady's head in her lap. The Doctor poured something into her mouth, but all I heard was, "She is not dead." Then I was led off by a man to a little distance. After a while the lady was taken to the carriage, and we came home together. I heard my master say to a gentleman who stopped him to inquire, that he hoped no bones were broken, but that she had not spoken yet.'

When Lord George took Ginger for hunting, York shook his head; he said it ought to be a steady hand to train a horse for the first season, and not a random rider like Lord George.

Ginger used to like it very much, but sometimes when she came back I could see that she had been very much strained, and now and then she gave a short cough. She had too much spirit to complain, but I could not help feeling anxious about her.

Two days after the accident Blantyre paid me a visit. He patted me and praised me very much and told Lord George that he was sure the horse knew of Annie's danger as well as he did. 'I could not have held him in if I would,' said he; 'she ought never to ride any other horse.'

I found by their conversation that my young mistress was now out of danger and would soon be able to ride again. This was good news to me, and I looked forward to a happy life.

CHAPTER TWENTY-FIVE

REUBEN SMITH

I MUST now say a little about Reuben Smith, who was left in charge of the stables when York went to London. No one more thoroughly understood his business than he did, and when he was all right, there could not be a more faithful or valuable man. He was gentle and very clever in his management of horses, and could doctor them almost as well as a farrier, for he had lived two years with a veterinary surgeon. He was a first-rate driver, and could take a four-in-hand, or a tandem, as easily as a pair.

He was a handsome man, a good scholar, and had very pleasant manners. I believe everybody liked him; certainly the horses did. The only wonder was that he should be in an under situation, and not in the place of a head coachman like York: but he had one great fault—the love of drink. He was not like some men, always at it; he used to keep steady for weeks or months together; but then he would break out and have a 'bout' of it, as York called it, and be a disgrace to himself, a terror to his wife, and a nuisance to all that had to do with him. He was, however, so useful that two or three times York had hushed the matter up, and kept it from the Earl's knowledge.

It was now early in April, and the family was expected home some time in May. The light brougham was to be fresh done up, and as Colonel Blantyre was obliged to return to his regiment, it was arranged that Smith should drive him to the town in it, and then ride back; for this purpose he took the saddle with him, and I was chosen for the journey.

At the station the Colonel put some money into Smith's hand and bade him good-bye, saying: 'Take care of your young mistress, Reuben, and don't let Black Auster be hacked about by any random young prig that wants to ride him—keep him for the lady.'

We left the carriage at the maker's, and Smith drove me to the White Lion, and ordered the ostler to feed me well and have me ready for him at four o'clock. A nail in one of my front shoes had started as I came along, but the ostler did not notice it till just about four o'clock. Smith did not come into the yard till five, and then he said he should not leave till six, as he had met with some old friends. The man then told him of the nail, and asked if he should have the shoe looked to.

'No,' said Smith, 'that will be all right till we get home.'

He spoke in a very loud, off-hand way, and I thought it was very unlike him not to see about the shoe, as he was generally wonderfully particular about loose nails in our shoes. He came neither at six, seven, nor eight, and it was nearly nine o'clock before he called me, and then it was with a loud, rough voice. He seemed in a very bad temper and abused the ostler, though I could not tell what for.

The landlord stood at the door, and said, 'Have a care, Mr. Smith!' but he answered angrily with an oath; and almost before he was out of the town he began to gallop, frequently giving me a sharp cut with his whip, though I was going at full speed. The moon had not yet risen, and it was very dark. Having been recently mended, the roads were stony, and going over them at this pace made my shoe looser, so that when we were near the turnpike gate it came off.

If Smith had been in his right senses he would have been sensible of something wrong in my pace; but he was too madly drunk to notice anything.

Beyond the turnpike was a long piece of road, upon which some fresh stones had just been laid—large, sharp stones, over which no horse could be driven quickly without risk of danger. Over this road, with one shoe gone, I was forced to gallop at my utmost speed, my rider meanwhile cutting into me with his whip, and with wild curses urging me to go still faster. Of course my shoeless foot suffered dreadfully; the hoof was broken and split down to the quick, and the inside was terribly cut by the sharpness of the stones.

This could not go on; no horse could keep his footing under such circumstances as the pain was too great. I stumbled, and fell with violence on both my knees. Smith was flung off by my fall, and, owing to the speed at which I was going, he must have fallen with great force. I soon recovered my feet and limped to the side of the road, where it was free from stones.

The moon had just risen above the hedge, and by its light I could see Smith lying a few yards beyond me. After making one slight effort to rise, there was a heavy groan. He did not move. I could have groaned too, for I was suffering intense pain both from my foot and knees; but horses are used to bear their pain in silence. I uttered no sound, but stood there and listened.

One more heavy groan from Smith; but though he now lay in the full moonlight, I could see no motion. I could do nothing for him nor for myself. But, oh! how I listened for the sound of horse, or wheels, or footsteps. The road was not much frequented, and at this time of the night we might stay for hours before help came to us.

I stood watching and listening. It was a calm, sweet April night; there were no sounds except a few low notes of a nightingale; and nothing moved but the white clouds near the moon, and a brown owl that flitted over the hedge. It made me think of the summer nights long ago, when I used to lie beside my mother in the green, pleasant meadow at Farmer Grey's.

CHAPTER TWENTY-SIX

HOW IT ENDED

IT must have been nearly midnight when I heard at a great distance the sound of a horse's feet. Sometimes the sound died away, then it grew clearer again and nearer. The road to Earlshall led through plantations that belonged to the Earl; the sound came in that direction, and I hoped it might be some one coming in search of us. As the sound came nearer and nearer, I was almost sure I could distinguish Ginger's step; a little nearer still, and I could tell she was in the dog-cart. I neighed loudly, and was overjoyed to hear an answering neigh from Ginger and men's voices. They came slowly over the stones, and stopped at the dark figure that lay upon the ground.

One of the men jumped out, and stooped down over it. 'It is Reuben!' he said, 'and he does not stir.'

The other man followed and bent over him. 'He's dead,' he said; 'feel how cold his hands are.'

They raised him up, but there was no life, and his hair was soaked with blood. Laying him down again, they came and looked at me and saw my cut knees.

'Why, the horse has been down and has thrown him! Who would have thought the black horse would have done that? Nobody thought he could fall. Reuben must have been lying here for hours! Odd, too, that the horse has not moved from the place.'

Robert then attempted to lead me forward. I made a step, but almost fell again.

'Hallo! he's bad in his foot as well as his knees. Look here—his hoof is cut all to pieces; he might well come down, poor fellow! I tell you what, Ned, I'm afraid it hasn't been all right with Reuben! Just think of him riding a horse over these stones without a shoe! Why, if he had been in his right senses, he would just as soon have tried to ride him over the moon. I'm afraid it has been the old thing over again.

'Poor Susan! she looked awfully pale when she came to my house to ask if he had come home. She made me believe he was not a bit anxious, and talked of a lot of things that might have kept him. But for all that, she begged me to go and meet him. But what must we do? There's the horse to get home as well as the body—and that will be no easy matter.'

Then followed a conversation between them, till it was agreed that Robert, the groom, should lead me, and that Ned should take the body; it was a hard job to get it into the dog-cart, for there was no one to hold Ginger; but she knew as well as I did what was going on, and stood as still as a stone. I noticed that, because, if she had a fault it was that she was impatient in standing.

Ned started off very slowly with his sad load, and Robert

came and looked at my foot again; then he took his handkerchief and bound it closely round, and so led me home. I shall never forget that night walk; it was more than three miles. Robert led me on very slowly, and I limped and hobbled on as well as I could, suffering great pain. I am sure he was sorry for me, for he often patted and encouraged me, talking to me in a pleasant voice.

At last I reached my own box and had some corn; and after Robert had wrapped up my knees in wet cloths, he tied up my foot in a bran poultice to draw out the heat, and to cleanse it before the horse doctor saw it in the morning. Then I managed to get myself down on the straw and slept in spite of the pain.

The next day, after the farrier had examined my wounds, he said he hoped the joint was not injured, and if so, I should not be spoiled for work, but I should never lose the blemish. I believe they did the best to make a good cure, but it was a long and painful one. Proud flesh, as they called it, came up in my knees, and was burnt out with caustic; and when at last my knees were healed, they put a blistering fluid over the front of both to bring off all the hair; they had some reason for this, and I suppose it was all right.

As Smith's death had been so sudden, and no one was there to see it, there was an inquest held. The landlord and ostler at the White Lion with several other people, gave evidence that he was intoxicated when he started from the inn; the keeper of the toll-gate said he rode at a hard gallop through the gate; and my shoe was picked up amongst the stones; so the case was quite plain to them, and I was cleared of all blame.

Everybody pitied Susan; she was nearly out of her mind, and kept saying over and over again, 'Oh! he was so good—so good! It was all that cursed drink; why will they sell that cursed drink? Oh, Reuben, Reuben!' So she went on till after he was buried; and then, as she had no home or relations, she, with her six little children, were obliged once more to leave the pleasant home by the tall oak-trees, and go into that great gloomy Union House.

CHAPTER TWENTY-SEVEN

RUINED, AND GOING DOWNHILL

As soon as my knees were sufficiently healed, I was turned into a small meadow for a month or two. No other creature was there, and though I enjoyed the liberty and the sweet grass, yet I had been so long used to society that I felt very lonely. Ginger and I had become fast friends, and now I missed her company extremely.

I often neighed when I heard horses' feet passing in the road, but I seldom got an answer, till one morning the gate was opened, and who should come in but poor old Ginger! The man slipped off her halter and left her there. With a joyful whinny I trotted up to her; we were both glad to meet, but I soon found that it was not for our pleasure that she was brought to be with me. Her story would be too long to tell, but the end of it was that she had been ruined by hard riding, and was now turned off to see what rest would do.

Lord George was young and would take no warning. He was a hard rider, and would hunt whenever he could get a chance, quite careless of his horse. Soon after I left the stable there was a steeplechase, and he determined to ride. Though the groom told him the mare was a little strained, and was not fit for the race, he did not believe it, and on the day of the race he urged Ginger to keep up with the foremost riders. With her high spirit, she strained herself to the utmost and came in with the first three horses; but her wind was touched, besides which, he was too heavy for her, and her back was strained.

'And so,' she said, 'here we are, ruined in the prime of our youth and strength—you by a drunkard, and I by a fool; it is very hard.'

We both felt in ourselves that we were not what we had been. However that did not spoil the pleasure we had in each other's company. We did not gallop about as we once did, but we used

85

to feed and lie down together, and stand for hours under one of the shady lime-trees with our heads close to each other; and so we passed our time till the family returned from town.

One day we saw the Earl come into the meadow, and York was with him. Seeing who it was, we stood still under our lime-tree, and let them come up to us. They examined us carefully. The Earl seemed much annoyed.

'There is three hundred pounds flung away for no earthly use,' said he; 'but what I care most for is, that these horses of my old friend, who thought they would find a good home with me, are ruined. The mare shall have a twelve-months' run, and we shall see what that will do for her; but the black one must be sold; 'tis a great pity, but I could not have knees like these in my stables.'

'No, my lord, of course not,' said York, 'but he might get a place where appearance is not of much consequence, and still be well treated. I know a man in Bath, the master of some livery stables, who often wants a good horse at a low figure; I know he looks well after his horses. The inquest cleared the horse's character, and your lordship's recommendation or mine would be sufficient warrant for him.'

'You had better write to him, York. I should be more particular about the place than the money he would fetch.'

After this they left us.

'They'll soon take you away,' said Ginger, 'and I shall lose the only friend I have, and most likely we shall never see each other again. 'Tis a hard world!'

About a week after this, Robert came into the field with a halter, which he slipped over my head and led me away. There was no leave-taking of Ginger; we neighed to each other as I was led off, and she trotted anxiously along by the hedge, calling to me as long as she could hear the sound of my feet.

Through the recommendation of York, I was bought by the master of the livery stables. I had to go by train, a new experience to me, requiring a good deal of courage the first time; but as I found the puffing, rushing, whistling, and more than all, the trembling of the horse-box in which I stood, did me no real harm, I soon took it quietly.

When I reached the end of my journey, I found myself in a tolerably comfortable stable and well attended to. These stables were not so airy and pleasant as those I had been used to. The stalls were laid on a slope instead of being level, and as my head was kept tied to the manger, I was obliged always to stand on the slope, which was very fatiguing. Men do not seem to know yet that horses can do more work if they can stand comfortably and can turn about.

However, I was well fed and well cleaned, and, on the whole, I think our master took as much care of us as he could. He kept a good many horses and carriages of different kinds, for hire. Sometimes his own men drove them; at others the horse and chaise were let to gentlemen or ladies who drove themselves.

CHAPTER TWENTY-EIGHT

A JOB HORSE AND ITS DRIVERS

HITHERTO I had always been driven by people who at least knew how to drive; but in this place I was to get my experience of all the different kinds of bad and ignorant driving to which we horses are subjected; for I was a 'job-horse,' and was let out to all sorts of people who wished to hire me; and as I was good-tempered and gentle, I think I was more often let out to the ignorant drivers than some of the other horses, because I could be depended upon. It would take a long time to tell of all the different styles in which I was driven, but I will mention a few of them.

First, there were the tight-rein drivers—men who seemed to think that all depended on holding the reins as hard as they could, never relaxing the pull on the horse's mouth or giving him the least liberty of movement. These are always talking about 'keeping the horse well in hand,' and 'holding a horse up,' just as if a horse was not made to hold himself up.

Some poor broken-down horses, whose mouths have been made hard and insensible by just such drivers as these, may, perhaps, find some support in it; but for a horse who can depend upon its own legs, has a tender mouth, and is easily guided, it is not only tormenting, but stupid.

Then there are the loose-rein drivers, who let the reins lie easily on our backs and their own hand rest lazily on their knees. Of course, such gentlemen have no control over a horse, if anything happens suddenly. If a horse shies, starts, or stumbles, they are nowhere, and cannot help the horse or themselves till the mischief is done.

Of course, for myself, I had no objection to it, as I was not in the habit of either starting or stumbling, and had only been used to depend on my driver for guidance and encouragement; still, one likes to feel the rein a little in going downhill, and likes to know that one's driver has not gone to sleep.

Besides, a slovenly way of driving gets a horse into bad, and often lazy, habits; and when he changes hands he has to be whipped out of them with more or less pain and trouble. Squire Gordon always kept us to our best pace and our best manners. He said that spoiling a horse and letting him get into bad habits was just as cruel as spoiling a child, and both had to suffer for it afterwards.

Moreover, these drivers are often altogether careless, and will attend to anything else rather than to their horses. I went out in the phaeton one day with one of them; he had a lady and two children behind. He flopped the reins about as we started, and, of course, gave me several unmeaning cuts with the whip, though I was fairly off. There had been a good deal of road-mending going on, and even where the stones were not freshly laid down there was a great many loose ones about. My driver was laughing and joking with the lady and the children, and talking about the country to the right and to the left; but he never thought it worth while to keep an eye on his horse, or to drive on the smoothest parts of the road; and so it easily happened that I got a stone in one of my fore feet.

Now, if Mr. Gordon or John, or, in fact, any good driver, had been there, he would have seen that something was wrong before I had gone three paces. Or, even if it had been dark, a practised hand would have felt by the rein that there was something wrong in the step, and would have got down and picked out the stone. But this man went on laughing and talking, whilst at every step the stone became more firmly wedged between my shoe and the frog of my foot. The stone was sharp on the inside and round on the outside, which, as every one knows, is the most dangerous kind that a horse can pick up, as it cuts his foot and at the same time makes him most liable to stumble and fall.

Whether the man was partly blind or only very careless, I can't say; but he drove me with that stone in my foot for a good half mile before he saw anything was wrong. By that time I was going so lame with the pain that at last he saw it, and called out, 'Well, here's a go! Why, they have sent us out with a lame horse! What a shame!'

He then jerked the reins and flipped about with the whip, saying, 'Now, then, it's no use playing the old soldier with me; there's the journey to go, and it's no use turning lame and lazy.'

Just at this time a farmer came riding up on a brown cob; he lifted his hat and pulled up.

'I beg your pardon, sir,' he said, 'but I think there is something the matter with your horse; he goes very much as if he had a stone in his shoe. If you will allow me, I will look at his feet; these loose, scattered stones are very dangerous things for the horses.'

'He's a hired horse,' said the driver. 'I don't know what's the matter with him, but it's a great shame to send out a lame beast like this.'

The farmer dismounted, and, slipping his rein over his arm, at once took up my near foot.

'Bless me, there's a stone. Lame! I should think so!'

At first he tried to dislodge it with his hand, but as it was now very tightly wedged, he drew a stone-pick out of his pocket, and very carefully, and with some trouble, got it out. Then, holding it up, he said, 'there, that's the stone your horse has picked up; it is a wonder he did not fall down and break his knees into the bargain!'

'Well, to be sure!' said my driver. 'That is a queer thing; I never knew before that horses picked up stones.'

'Didn't you?' said the farmer rather contemptuously; 'but they do, though, and the best of them will do it, and can't help it sometimes on such roads as these. And if you don't want to lame your horse, you must look sharp and get them out quickly. This foot is very much bruised,' he said, setting it gently down and patting me. 'If I may advise, sir, you had better drive him gently for a while; the foot is a good deal hurt, and the lameness will not go off directly.'

Then, mounting his cob, and raising his hat to the lady, he drove off.

When he was gone, my driver began to flop the reins about and whip the harness, by which I understood that I was to go on, which of course I did, glad that the stone was gone, but still in a good deal of pain.

This was the sort of experience we job-horses often had.

CHAPTER TWENTY-NINE

COCKNEYS

THEN there is the steam-engine style of driving; these drivers were mostly people from towns, who never had a horse of their own, and generally travelled by rail.

They always seemed to think that a horse was something like a steam-engine only smaller. At any rate, they think that if only they pay for it, a horse is bound to go just as far, and just as fast, and with just as heavy a load, as they please. And be the roads heavy and muddy, or dry and good, be they stony or smooth, uphill or downhill, it is all the same—on, on, one must go at the same pace, with no relief and no consideration.

These people never think of getting out to walk up a steep hill. Oh, no, they have paid to ride, and ride they will! The horse? Oh, he's used to it! What were horses made for, if not to drag people uphill? Walk! A good joke, indeed! And so the whip is plied, and the rein is jerked, and often a rough, scolding voice cries out, 'Go along, you lazy beast!' And then comes another slash of the whip, when all the time we are doing our very best to get along, uncomplaining and obedient, though often sorely harassed and down-hearted.

This steam-engine style of driving wears us up faster than any other kind. I would far rather go twenty miles with a good, considerate driver than ten with some of these; it would take less out of me.

Another thing—they scarcely ever put on the drag, however steep the hill may be, and thus bad accidents sometimes happen; or if they do put it on, they often forget to take it off at the bottom of the hill; and more than once I have had to pull half-way up the next hill with one of the wheels lodged fast in the drag-shoe before my driver chose to think about it; and that is a terrible strain on a horse.

Then these Cockneys, instead of starting at an easy pace as a gentleman would do, generally set off at full speed from the very stable yard; and when they want to stop, they first whip us and then pull up so suddenly that we are nearly thrown on our haunches, and our mouths are jagged with the bit; they call that pulling up with a dash! And when they turn a corner they do it as sharply as if there was no right side or wrong side of the road.

I well remember one spring evening. Rory and I had been out for the day (Rory was the horse that mostly went with me when a pair was ordered, and a good, honest fellow he was). We had our own driver, and, as he was always considerate and gentle with us, we had a very pleasant day. About twilight we were coming home at a good smart pace. Our road turned sharp to the left; but as we were close to the hedge on our own side, and there was plenty of room to pass, our driver did not pull us in. As we neared the corner I heard a horse and two wheels coming rapidly down the hill towards us. The hedge was high, and I could see nothing; but the next moment we were upon each other. Happily for me, I was on the side next the hedge. Rory was on the right side of the pole, and had not even a shaft to protect him.

The man who was driving was making straight for the corner, and when he came in sight of us he had no time to pull over to his own side. The whole shock came upon Rory. The gig shaft ran right into his chest making him stagger back with a cry that I shall never forget. The other horse was thrown upon its haunches, and one shaft broken. It turned out that it was a horse from our own stables, with the high-wheeled gig that the young men were so fond of.

The driver was one of those random, ignorant fellows, who don't even know which is their own side of the road, or, if they know, don't care. And there was poor Rory, with his flesh torn open and bleeding and the blood streaming down. They said if it had been a little more to one side, it would have killed him; and a good thing for him, poor fellow, if it had.

As it was, it was a long time before the wound healed, and then he was sold for coal carting; and what that is, up and down those steep hills, only horses know. Some of the sights I saw there, where a horse can come downhill with a heavily loaded two-wheeled cart behind him, on which no drag could be placed, make me sad even now to think of.

After Rory was disabled I often went in the carriage with a mare named Peggy, who stood in the stall next to mine. She was a strong, well-made animal, of a bright dun colour, beautifully dappled, and with a dark-brown mane and tail. There was no high-breeding about her, but she was very pretty, and remarkably sweet-tempered and willing. Still, there was an anxious look about her eye, by which I knew that she had some trouble. The first time we went out together I thought she had a very odd pace; she seemed to go partly in a trot, partly in a canter—three or four paces, and then to make a little jump forward.

It was very unpleasant for any horse who pulled with her, and made me quite fidgety. When we got home, I asked her what made her go in that odd, awkward way.

'Ah,' she said in a troubled manner, 'I know my paces are very bad, but what can I do? It really is not my fault, it is just because my legs are so short. I stand nearly as high as you, but your legs are a good three inches longer above your knees than mine, and of course you can take a much longer step, and go much faster. You see, I did not make myself; I wish I could have done so, I would have had long legs then; all my troubles come from my short legs,' said Peggy, in a desponding tone.

'But how is it,' I said, 'when you are so strong and good-tempered and willing?'

'Why, you see,' said she, 'men will go so fast, and if one can't keep up to other horses, it is nothing but whip, whip, whip, all the time. And so I have had to keep up as I could, and have got into this ugly, shuffling pace. It was not always so; when I lived with my first master I always went a good regular trot, but then he was not in such a hurry. He was a young clergyman in the country, and a good, kind master he was. He had two churches a good way apart, and a great deal of work, but he never scolded or whipped me for not going fast. He was very fond of me. I only wish I was with him now; but he had to leave and go to a large town, and then I was sold to a farmer.

'Some farmers, you know, are capital masters; but I think this one was a low sort of man. He cared nothing about good horses or good driving; he only cared for going fast. I went as fast as I could, but that would not do, and he was always whipping; so I got into this way of making a spring forward to keep up. On market nights he used to stay very late at the inn, and then drive home at a gallop.

'One dark night he was galloping home as usual when all of a sudden the wheel came against some great, heavy thing in the road, and turned the gig over in a minute. He was thrown out and his arm broken, and some of his ribs, I think. At any rate, it was the end of my living with him, and I was not sorry. But you see it will be the same everywhere for me, if men *must* go so fast. I wish my legs were longer!'

Poor Peggy! I was very sorry for her, and I could not comfort her, for I knew how hard it was upon slow-paced horses to be put with fast ones; all the whipping comes to their share, and they can't help it.

She was often used in the phaeton, and was very much liked by some of the ladies, because she was so gentle; and some time after this she was sold to two ladies who drove themselves, and wanted a safe, good horse.

I met her several times out in the country, going a good, steady pace, and looking as gay and contented as a horse could be. I was very glad to see her, for she deserved a good place.

Of course we sometimes came in for good driving here. I remember one morning I was put into the light gig, and taken to a house in Pulteney Street. Two gentlemen came out; the taller of them came round to my head. He looked at the bit and bridle, and just shifted the collar with his hand, to see if it fitted comfortably.

'Do you consider this horse wants a curb?' he said to the ostler.

'Well,' said the man, 'I should say he would go just as well without for he has an uncommonly good mouth, and though he has a fine spirit, he has no vice; but we generally find people like the curb.'

'I don't like it,' said the gentleman; 'be so good as to take it off, and put the rein in at the cheek. An easy mouth is a great thing on a long journey, is it not, old fellow?' he said, patting my neck.

Then he took the reins, and they both got up. I can remember now how quietly he turned me round, and then with a light feel of the rein, and a gentle drawing of the whip across my back, we were off.

I arched my neck and set off at my best pace. I found I had some one behind me who knew how a good horse ought to be driven. It seemed like old times again, and made me feel quite gay.

This gentleman took a great liking to me, and after trying me several times with the saddle, he prevailed upon my master to sell me to a friend of his who wanted a safe, pleasant horse for riding. And so it came to pass that in the summer I was sold to Mr. Barry.

CHAPTER THIRTY

A THIEF

My new master was an unmarried man. He lived at Bath, and was much engaged in business. His doctor advised him to take horse exercise, and for this purpose he bought me. He hired a stable a short distance from his lodgings, and engaged a man named Filcher as groom. My master knew very little about horses, but he treated me well, and I should have had a good and easy place but for circumstances of which he was ignorant. He ordered the best hay, with plenty of oats, crushed beans, and bran, with vetches or rye grass, as the man might think needful. I heard the master give the order, so I knew there was plenty of good food, and I thought I was well off.

For a few days all went on well; I found that my groom understood his business. He kept the stable clean and airy, groomed me thoroughly, and was never otherwise than gentle. He had been an ostler in one of the great hotels in Bath. This he had given up, and now cultivated fruit and vegetables for the market; and his wife reared and fattened poultry and rabbits for sale.

After a while it seemed to me that my oats became very short. I had the beans, but bran was mixed with them with a few oats; certainly there were not more than a quarter of the oats there should have been. In two or three weeks this began to tell upon my strength and spirits. The grass food, though very good, was not the thing without corn to keep up my condition. However, I could not complain nor make known my wants. So it went on for about two months; and I wondered my master did not see that something was the matter.

However, one afternoon he rode out into the country to see a friend of his—a gentleman farmer who lived on the road to Wells. This gentleman had a very quick eye for horses; and after he had welcomed his friend, casting his eye over me, he said:—

'It seems to me, Barry, that your horse does not look so well as he did when you first had him: has he been well?'

'Yes, I believe so,' said my master, 'but he is not nearly so lively as he was. My groom tells me that horses are always dull and weak in the autumn, and that I must expect it.'

'Autumn! fiddlestick!' said the farmer; 'why, this is only August; and with your light work and good food, he ought not to go down like this, even if it were autumn. How do you feed him?'

My master told him. The other shook his head slowly, and began to feel me over.

'I can't say who eats your corn, my dear fellow, but I am much mistaken if your horse gets it. Have you ridden very fast?'

'No, very gently.'

'Then just put your hand here,' said he, passing his hand over my neck and shoulders; 'he is as warm and damp as a horse just come up from grass. I advise you to look into your stable a little more. I hate to be suspicious, and, thank Heaven, I have no cause to be, for I can trust my men, present or absent; but there are mean scoundrels wicked enough to rob a dumb beast of his food. You must look into it.' And turning to his man who had come to take me, 'Give this horse a good feed of bruised oats, and don't stint him.'

'Dumb beasts!' yes, we are; but if I could have spoken, I could have told my master where his oats went to. My groom used to come every morning about six o'clock with a little boy, who always had a covered basket with him. The boy used to go with his father into the harness-room, where the corn was kept, and I could see them, when the door stood ajar, fill a little bag with oats out of the bin, and then the boy used to be off.

Five or six mornings after this, just as the boy had left the stable, the door was pushed open and a policeman walked in, holding the child tight by the arm. Another policeman followed, and locked the door on the inside, saying, 'Show me the place where your father keeps his rabbits' food.'

The boy looked very frightened and began to cry; but there was no escape; and he led the way to the corn-bin. Here the policeman found another empty bag like that which was found full of oats in the boy's basket.

Filcher was cleaning my feet at the time, but they soon saw him and though he blustered a good deal, they walked him off to the 'lock-up,' and his boy with him. I heard afterwards that the boy was not held to be guilty, but the man was sentenced to prison for two months.

CHAPTER THIRTY-ONE

A HUMBUG

MY master was not immediately suited, but in a few days my new groom came. He was a tall, good-looking fellow enough; but if ever there was a humbug in the shape of a groom, Alfred Smirk was the man. He was very civil to me, and never used me ill; in fact, he did a great deal of stroking and patting, when his master was there to see it. To make me look smart he always brushed my mane and tail with water, and my hoofs with oil, before he brought me to the door, but as to clearing my feet, looking to my shoes, or grooming me thoroughly, he thought no more of these than if I had been a cow. He left my bit rusty, my saddle damp, and my crupper stiff.

Alfred Smirk considered himself very handsome; he spent a great deal of time before a little looking-glass in the harness-room, attending to his hair, whiskers, and necktie. When his master was speaking to him, it was always, 'Yes, sir; yes, sir,' touching his hat at every word; and every one thought he was a very nice young man, and that Mr. Barry was very fortunate to meet with him. I should say he was the laziest, most conceited fellow I ever came near.

Of course it was a great thing not to be ill-used, but then a horse wants more than that. I had a loose-box, and might have been very comfortable if he had not been too indolent to clean it out. He never took all the straw away, and the smell from what lay underneath was very bad, while the strong vapours that rose up from it made my eyes smart and inflame, and I had not the same appetite for my food.

One day my master came in and said: 'Alfred, the stable smells rather strong; should you not give that stall a good scrub, and throw down plenty of water?'

'Well, sir,' he said, touching his cap, 'I'll do so if you please, sir, but it is rather dangerous, sir, throwing down water in a horse's box; horses are very apt to take cold, sir. I should not like to do him an injury; but I'll do it if you please, sir.'

'Well,' said his master, 'I should not like him to take cold, but I don't like the smell of this stable; do you think the drains are all right?'

'Well, sir, now you mention it, I think the drain does sometimes send back a smell; there may be something wrong, sir.'

'Then send for the bricklayer and have it seen to,' said his master.

'Yes, sir, I will.'

The bricklayer came and pulled up a great many bricks, and found nothing amiss; so he put down some lime and charged the master five shillings; but the smell in my box was as bad as ever. This was not all. Standing as I did on a quantity of moist straw, my feet grew unhealthy and tender and the master used to say:—

'I don't know what is the matter with this horse, he goes very fumble-footed. I am sometimes afraid he will stumble.'

'Yes, sir,' said Alfred, 'I have noticed the same myself, when I have exercised him.'

Now the fact was that he hardly ever did exercise me, and when the master was busy, I often stood for days together without stretching my legs at all, and yet was fed just as high as if I were at hard work. This often disordered my health, and made me sometimes heavy and dull, but more often restless and feverish.

He never even gave me a meal of green meat or a bran mash, which would have cooled me, for he was altogether as ignorant as he was conceited; and then, instead of exercise or change of food, I had to take horse balls and draughts; which, beside the nuisance of having them poured down my throat, used to make me feel ill and uncomfortable.

One day my feet were so tender that, trotting over some fresh stones with my master on my back, I made two such serious stumbles that as we came down Lansdown into the city, master stopped at the farrier's and asked him to see what was the matter with me. The man took up my feet one by one and examined them; then standing up and dusting his hands one against the other, he said:—

'Your horse has got the "thrush," and badly, too; his feet are very tender; it is fortunate that he has not been down. I wonder your groom has not seen to it before. This is the sort of thing we find in foul stables where the litter is never properly cleared out. If you will send him here to-morrow I will attend to the hoof, and I will direct your man how to apply some liniment which I will give him.'

The next day I had my feet thoroughly cleansed and stuffed with tow soaked in some strong lotion, and a very unpleasant business it was.

The farrier ordered all the litter to be taken out of my box day by day, and the floor was to be kept very clean. Then I was to have bran mashes, a little green meat, and not so much corn, till my feet were well again. With this treatment I soon regained my spirits, but Mr. Barry was so much disgusted at being twice deceived by his grooms that he determined to give up keeping a horse and to hire when he wanted one. I was therefore kept till my feet were quite sound, and was then sold again.

CHAPTER THIRTY-TWO

A HORSE FAIR

No doubt a horse fair is a very amusing place to those who have nothing to lose; at any rate, there is plenty to see—long strings of young horses out of the country, fresh from the marshes; droves of shaggy little Welsh ponies, no higher than

Merrylegs; hundreds of cart horses of all sorts, some of them with their long tails braided up and tied with scarlet cord; and a good many, like myself, handsome and high-bred, but fallen into the middle class through some accident or blemish, unsoundness of wind, or some other complaint.

There were some splendid animals quite in their prime and fit for anything, who were throwing out their legs and showing off their paces in high style as they were trotted out with a leading rein, the groom running by the side. But round in the background were a number of poor things, sadly broken down with hard work, their knees knuckling over, and their hind legs swinging out at every step; some were very dejected-looking old horses, with the upper lip hanging down and the ears laying back heavily, as if there was no pleasure in life and no more hope; again, some were so thin you could see all their ribs; and some had old sores on their backs and hips. These were sad sights for a horse who knows not but that he may come to the same sad state.

There was a great deal of bargaining, running up and beating down; and if a horse may speak his mind so far as he understands, I should say there were more lies told and more trickery carried on at that horse fair than a clever man could give an account of. I was put with two or three other strong, useful-looking horses, and a good many people came to look at us. The gentlemen always turned from me when they saw my broken knees, though the man who had me swore it was only a slip in the stall.

To examine me, buyers began to pull my mouth open, then to look at my eyes, next to feel all the way down my legs, and to give me a hard feel of the skin and flesh, and, lastly, to try my paces. What a difference there was in the way these things were done! Some did it in a rough, offhand way, as if one was only a piece of wood; while others would take their hands gently over one's body, with a pat now and then, as much as to say, 'By your leave.' Of course, I judged the buyers a good deal by their manners to myself.

There was one man of whom I thought that if he would buy me I should be happy. He was not a gentleman, nor yet one of the loud, flashy sort that called themselves so. He was a rather small man, but well made, and quick in all his motions. I knew in a moment by the way he handled me that he was used to horses; he spoke gently, and his grey eye had a kindly, cheery look in it. It may seem strange—but it is true all the same —that the clean, fresh smell there was about him made me take to him. There was no smell of old beer and tobacco, which I hated, but a fresh smell as if he had come out of a hay-loft. He offered twenty-three pounds for me; but that was refused, and he walked away. I looked after him, but he was gone.

A very hard-looking, loud-voiced man came next. I was dreadfully afraid he would have me; but he walked off. One or two more came who did not mean business. Then the hard-faced man came back again and offered twenty-three pounds. A very close bargain was being driven, for my salesman began to think he should not get all he asked, and must come down; but just then the grey-eyed man came back again. I could not help reaching out my head towards him. He stroked my face kindly.

'Well, old chap,' he said, 'I think we should suit each other. I'll give twenty-four for him.'

'Say twenty-five and you shall have him.'

'Twenty-four ten,' said my friend, in a very decided tone, 'and not another sixpence—yes or no?'

'Done,' said the salesman, 'and you may depend upon it there's a monstrous deal of quality in that horse, and if you want him for cab work, he's a bargain.'

The money was paid on the spot, and my new master took my halter and led me out of the fair to an inn, where he had a saddle and bridle ready. He gave me a good feed of oats, and stood by whilst I ate it, talking to himself and talking to me. Half an hour after we were on our way to London, through pleasant lanes and country roads, until we came into the great London thoroughfare, on which we travelled steadily till in the twilight we reached the great City. The gas lamps were already lighted; there were streets to the right, streets to the left, and streets crossing each other for mile upon mile. I thought we should never come to the end of them. At last, in passing through one, we came to a long cab-stand, when my rider called out in a cheery voice, 'Good-night, Governor!'

'Hallo!' cried a voice, 'have you got a good one?'

'I think so,' replied my owner.

'I wish you luck with him.'

'Thank ye, Governor'; and he rode on. We soon turned up one of the side streets, and about half-way up turned again into a very narrow one, with rather poor-looking houses on one side and what seemed to be coach-houses and stables on the other.

My owner pulled up at one of the houses and whistled. The door flew open, and a young woman, followed by a little girl and boy, ran out. There was a very lively greeting as my rider dismounted.

'Now, then, Harry, my boy, open the gates, and mother will bring us the lantern.'

The next minute they were all standing round me in a small stable yard.

'Is he gentle, father?'

'Yes, Dolly, as gentle as your own kitten; come and pat him.'

At once the little hand was patting about fearlessly all over my shoulder. How good it felt!

'Let me get him a bran mash while you rub him down,' said the mother.

'Do, Polly, it's just what he wants, and I know you've got a beautiful mash ready for me.'

'Sausage dumpling and apple turnover,' shouted the boy; this set them all laughing. I was led into a comfortable, clean-smelling stall, with plenty of dry straw, and, after a capital supper, I lay down, thinking I was going to be happy.

CHAPTER THIRTY-THREE

A LONDON CAB HORSE

My new master's name was Jeremiah Barker, but as every one called him Jerry, I shall do the same. Polly, his wife, was just as good a match as a man could have. She was a plump, trim, tidy, little woman, with smooth, dark hair, dark eyes, and a merry little mouth. The boy was nearly twelve years old—a tall, frank, good-tempered lad; and little Dorothy (Dolly they called her) was her mother over again at eight years old. They were all wonderfully fond of each other; I never, before or since, knew such a happy, merry family.

Jerry had a cab of his own and two horses, which he drove and attended to himself. His other horse was a tall, white, rather large-boned animal, called Captain. He was old now, but when he was young he must have been splendid; there was still the proud way of holding his head and arching his neck; in fact, he was a high-bred, fine-mannered, noble, old horse, every inch of him.

He told me that in his early youth he went to the Crimean War, for he belonged to an officer in the cavalry, and used to lead the regiment: I will tell more of that hereafter.

The next morning, when I was well groomed, Polly and Dolly came into the yard to see me and to make friends. Harry had been helping his father since the early morning, and had stated his opinion that I should turn out 'a regular brick.' Polly brought me a slice of apple, and Dolly a piece of bread, and they made as much of me as if I had been the 'Black Beauty' of olden time. To be petted again and talked to in a gentle voice was a great treat; and I let them see as well as I could that I wished to be friendly. Polly thought I was very handsome and a great deal too good for a cab, if it was not for the broken knees.

'Of course, there's no one to tell us whose fault that was,' said Jerry, 'and as long as I don't know, I shall give him the benefit of the doubt; for a firmer, neater stepper I never rode. We'll call him "Jack," after the old one—shall we, Polly?'

'Do,' she said, 'for I like to keep a good name going.'

Captain went out in the cab all the morning. Harry came in after school to feed me and give me water. In the afternoon I was put into the cab. Jerry took as much pains to see if the collar and bridle fitted comfortably as if he had been John Manly over again. When the crupper was let out a hole or two, it all fitted well. There was no bearing rein or curb, nothing but a plain ring snaffle. What a blessing that was!

After driving through the side-street we came to the large cab-stand where Jerry had said 'Good-night.' On one side of this wide street were high houses with wonderful shop fronts, and on the other was an old church, and churchyard surrounded by iron palisades. Alongside these iron rails a number of cabs were drawn up, waiting for passengers. Bits of hay were lying about on the ground. Some of the men were standing together talking; others were sitting on their boxes, reading the newspapers; and one or two were feeding their horses with bits of hay and a drink of water. We pulled up in the rank at the back of the last cab. Two or three men came round and began to look at me and to pass their remarks.

'Very good for a funeral,' said one.

'Too smart-looking,' said another, shaking his head in a very wise way; 'you'll find out something wrong one of these fine mornings, or my name isn't Jones.'

'Well,' said Jerry pleasantly, 'I suppose I need not find it out till it finds me out, eh? and, if so, I'll keep up my spirits a little longer.'

Then came up a broad-faced man dressed in a great grey coat with great grey capes and great white buttons, a grey hat, and a blue comforter loosely tied round his neck. His hair was grey too, but he was a jolly-looking fellow, and the other men made way for him. He looked me all over, as if he had been going to buy me; and then straightening himself up, he said with a grunt, 'He's the right sort for you, Jerry; I don't care what you gave for him, he'll be worth it.' Thus my character was established on the stand.

This man's name was Grant, but he was called 'Grey Grant,' or 'Governor Grant.' He had been the longest of any of the men on that stand, and he took it upon himself to settle matters and stop disputes. He was generally a good-humoured, sensible man; but if his temper was a little out, as it was sometimes when he had drunk too much, nobody liked to come too near his fist, for he could deal a very hard blow.

The first week of my life as a cab horse was very trying; I had never been used to London, and the noise, the hurry, the crowds of horses, carts, and carriages through which I had to make my way, made me feel anxious and harassed; but I soon found that I could perfectly trust my driver, and then I made myself easy and got used to it.

Jerry was as good a driver as I had ever known; and, what was better, he took as much thought for his horses as he did for himself. He soon found out that I was willing to work and to do my best; and he never laid the whip on me unless it was to draw the end of it gently over my back when I was to go on. Generally I knew this quite well by the way in which he took up the reins; and I believe his whip was more frequently stuck up by his side than in his hand.

In a short time my master and I understood each other as well as horse and man could do. In the stable, too, he did all that he could for our comfort. The stalls were of the old-fashioned style—too much on the slope; but he had two movable bars fixed across the back of our stalls, so that at night and when we were resting he just took off our halters and put up the bars, and thus we could turn about and stand whichever way we pleased; this is a great comfort.

Jerry kept us very clean, and gave us as much change of food as he could, and always plenty of it; and not only that, but he always gave us plenty of clean, fresh water, which he allowed to stand by us both night and day, except of course when we came in warm.

Some people say that a horse ought not to drink as much as he wishes; but I know if we are allowed to drink when we want it, we drink only a little at a time, and it does us a great deal more good than swallowing it down half a bucketful at a time, as we do if we have been left without water till we are thirsty and miserable.

Some grooms will go home to their beer and leave us for hours with our dry hay and oats, with nothing to moisten them; then, of course, we gulp down too much water at once, which helps to spoil our breathing and sometimes chills our stomachs.

But the best thing that we had here was our Sundays for rest. We worked so hard during the week that I do not think we could have kept up to it but for that day's rest; besides, we then had time to enjoy each other's company. It was on these days that I learned my companion's history.

CHAPTER THIRTY-FOUR

AN OLD WAR HORSE

CAPTAIN had been broken in and trained for an army horse, his first owner being an officer of cavalry going out to the Crimean War. He said he quite enjoyed the training with all the other horses—trotting together, turning together to the right hand or the left, halting at the word of command, or dashing forward at full speed at the sound of the trumpet, or signal of the officer. When young, he was a dark, dappled iron grey, and was considered very handsome. His master, a young, high-spirited gentleman, was very fond of him, and from the first treated him with the greatest care and kindness. He told me he thought the life of an army horse was very pleasant; but when it came to being sent abroad in a great ship over the sea, he almost changed his mind.

'That part of it' he said, 'was dreadful! Of course we could not walk off the land into the ship; so they were obliged to put strong straps under our bodies, and then we were lifted off our legs in spite of our struggles, and were swung through the air, over the water, to the deck of the great vessel. There we were placed in small, close stalls, and never for a long time saw the sky, or were we able to stretch our legs. The ship sometimes rolled about in high winds, and we were knocked about, and felt very ill. However, at last it came to an end, and we were hauled up, and swung over again to the land. We were very glad, and snorted and neighed for joy when we once more felt firm ground under our feet.

'We soon found that the country to which we had come was very different from our own, and that we had many hardships to endure besides the fighting; but many of the men were so fond of us that they did everything they could to make us comfortable, in spite of snow, wet, and the fact that all things were out of order.'

'But what about that fighting?' said I; 'was not that worse than anything else?'

'Well,' said he, 'I hardly know. We always liked to hear the trumpet sound, and to be called out, and were impatient to start off, though sometimes we had to stand for hours, waiting for the word of command. But when the word was given we used to spring forward as gaily and eagerly as if there were no cannon-balls, bayonets, or bullets. I believe so long as we felt our rider firm in the saddle, and his hand steady on the bridle, not one of us gave way to fear, not even when the terrible bombshells whirled through the air and burst into a thousand pieces.

'With my noble master, I went into many actions without a wound; and though I saw horses shot down with bullets, others pierced through with lances or gashed with fearful sabre-cuts, though I left them dead on the field, or dying in the agony of their wounds, I don't think I feared for myself. My master's cheery voice as he encouraged his men made me feel as if he and I could not be killed. I had such perfect trust in him, that whilst he was guiding me I was ready to charge up to the very cannon's mouth.

'I saw many brave men cut down, and many fall from their saddles mortally wounded. I have heard the cries and groans of the dying, cantered over ground slippery with blood, and frequently had to turn aside to avoid trampling on a wounded man or horse; but until one dreadful day, I had never felt terror: that day I shall never forget.'

Here old Captain paused for a while and drew a long breath; I waited, and he went on.

'It was one autumn morning, and, as usual, an hour before daybreak our cavalry had turned out ready caparisoned for the day's work, whether fighting or waiting. The men stood waiting by their horses, ready for orders. As the light increased there seemed to be some excitement among the officers; and before the day was well begun we heard the firing of the enemy's guns.

'Then one of the officers rode up and gave the word for the men to mount, and in a second every man was in his saddle, and every horse stood expecting the touch of the rein, or the pressure of his rider's heels—all animated, all eager. But still we had been trained so well, that, except by the champing of our bits, and by the restive tossing of our heads from time to time, it could not be said that we stirred.

'My dear master and I were at the head of the line, and as all sat motionless and watchful, he took a little stray lock of my mane which had turned over the wrong side, laid it over on the right and smoothed it down with his hand; then, patting my neck, he said: "We shall have a day of it to-day, Bayard, my beauty; but we'll do our duty as we always have done."

'That morning he stroked my neck more, I think, than he had ever done before; quietly on and on, as if he were thinking of something else. I loved to feel his hand on my neck, and arched my crest proudly and happily; but I stood very still, for I knew all his moods, and when he liked me to be quiet, and when gay.

'I cannot tell all that happened that day, but I will tell of the last charge that we made together; it was across a valley right in front of the enemy's cannon. By this time we were well used to the roar of heavy guns, the rattle of musket fire, and the firing of shot near us; but never had I been under such a fire as we rode through that day. From right, left, and front, shot and shell poured in upon us. Many a brave man went down, many a horse fell, flinging his rider to the earth; many a horse without a rider ran wildly out of the ranks; then, terrified at being alone with no hand to guide him, came pressing in amongst his old companions, to gallop with them to the charge.

'Fearful as it was, no one stopped, no one turned back. Every moment the ranks were thinned, but as our comrades fell we closed in to keep the others together; and instead of being shaken or staggered in our pace, our gallop became faster and faster as we neared the cannon, all clouded in white smoke, while the red fire flashed through it.

'My master, my dear master, was cheering on his comrades, with his right arm raised on high, when one of the balls, whizzing close to my head, struck him. I felt him stagger with the shock, though he uttered no cry. I tried to check my speed, but the sword dropped from his right hand, the rein fell loose from the left, and sinking backward from the saddle, he fell to the earth; the other riders swept past us, and by the force of their charge I was driven from the spot where he fell.

'I wanted to keep my place at his side, and not to leave him under that rush of horses' feet, but it was in vain. And now, without a master or a friend, I was alone on that great slaughter-ground. Then fear took hold of me, and I trembled as I had never trembled before. Then I, too, as I had seen others do, tried to join in the ranks and to gallop with them; but I was beaten off by the swords of the soldiers.

'Just then, a soldier whose horse had been killed under him caught at my bridle and mounted me, and with this new master I was again going forward. But our gallant company was cruelly overpowered, and those who remained alive after the fierce fight for the guns came galloping back over the same ground.

'Some of the horses had been so badly wounded that they could scarcely move from loss of blood; other noble creatures were trying on three legs to drag themselves along; and others were struggling to rise on their fore feet when their hind legs had been shattered by shot. Their groans were piteous to hear, and the beseeching look in their eyes as those who escaped passed by and left them to their fate I shall never forget. After the battle, the wounded men were brought in, and the dead were buried.'

'And what about the wounded horses?' I said; 'were they left to die?'

'No, the army farriers went over the field with their pistols, and shot all that were ruined. Some that had only slight wounds were brought back and attended to, but the greater part of the noble, willing creatures that went out that morning never came back! In our stables there was only about one in four that returned.

'I never saw my dear master again. I believe he fell dead from the saddle. Never did I love any other master so well. I went into many other engagements, but was only once wounded, and then not seriously; and when the war was over I came back again to England, as sound and strong as when I went out.'

I said, 'I have heard people talk about war as if it was a very fine thing.'

'Ah!' said he, 'I should think they have never seen it. No doubt it is very fine when there is no enemy, only just exercise, parade, and sham-fights. Yes, it is very fine then; but when thousands of good, brave men and horses are killed or crippled for life, then it has a very different look.'

'Do you know what they fought about?' said I.

'No,' he said, 'that is more than a horse can understand; but the enemy must have been awfully wicked people if it was right to go all that way over the sea on purpose to kill them.'

CHAPTER THIRTY-FIVE

JERRY BARKER

I NEVER knew a better man than my new master—kind and good, as strong for the right as John Manly, and so good-tempered and merry that very few people could pick a quarrel with him. He was very fond of making little songs, which he would sing to himself. His favourite was this:—

> '*Come, father and mother,*
> *And sister and brother,*
> *Come, all of you, turn to*
> *And help one another.*'

And so they did; Harry was as clever at stablework as a much older boy, and always wanted to do what he could. Then Polly and Dolly used to come in the morning to help with the cab—to brush and beat the cushions and rub the glass, while Jerry was giving us a cleaning in the yard and Harry was cleaning the harness. There used to be a great deal of laughing and fun between them, and it put Captain and me in much better spirits than if we had heard scolding and hard words. They were always early in the morning, for Jerry would say:—

> '*If you in the morning*
> *Throw minutes away,*
> *You can't pick them up*
> *In the course of the day.*
>
> *You may hurry and skurry,*
> *And flurry and worry,*
> *You've lost them for ever,*
> *For ever and aye.*'

He could not bear any careless loitering and waste of time; and nothing was so near making him angry as to find people who were always late wanting a cab horse to be driven hard to make up for their idleness.

One day two wild-looking young men came out of a tavern close by the stand, and called Jerry.

'Here, cabby! look sharp, we are rather late; put on the steam will you, and take us to Victoria in time for the one o'clock train. You shall have a shilling extra.'

'I will take you at the regular pace, gentlemen; shillings don't pay for putting on the steam like that.'

Larry's cab was standing next to ours. He flung open the door and said, 'I'm your man, gentlemen! Take my cab, my horse will get you there all right;' and as he shut them in, with a wink towards Jerry, he said, 'It's against his conscience to go beyond a jog-trot.' Then, slashing his jaded horse, he set off as hard as he could. Jerry patted me on the neck—'No, Jack, a shilling would not pay for that sort of thing, would it, old boy?'

Although Jerry was steadfastly set against hard driving to please careless people, he always went at a good fair pace, and was not against putting on the steam, as he said, if only he knew *why*.

I well remember one morning, as we were on the stand waiting for a fare, that a young man carrying a heavy portmanteau trod on a piece of orange-peel which lay on the pavement and fell down with great force.

Jerry was the first to run and lift him up. He seemed much stunned, and as they had led him into a shop, he walked as if he were in great pain. Jerry, of course, came back to the stand, but in about ten minutes one of the shopmen called him, so he drew up to the pavement.

'Can you take me to the South-Eastern Railway?' said the young man. 'This unlucky fall has made me late, I fear; but it is of great importance that I should not lose the twelve o'clock train. I should be most thankful if you could get me there in time, and will gladly pay you an extra fare.'

'I'll do my very best,' said Jerry heartily, 'if you think you are well enough, sir,' for he looked dreadfully white and ill.

'I *must* go,' he said earnestly. 'Please open the door, and let us lose no time.'

The next minute Jerry was on the box. He gave a cheery chirrup to me, and a twitch to the rein, that I well understood.

'Now then, Jack, my boy,' said he, 'spin along; we'll show them how we can get over the ground if we only know why.'

Jerry and I were used to the thickest traffic, and no one could beat us at getting through when we were set on it. I was quick and bold, and could always trust my driver; Jerry was quick and patient at the same time, and could trust his horse, which was a great thing too. He very seldom used the whip; I knew by his voice and his click, click, when he wanted to get on fast, and the rein told me where I was to go, so there was no need for whipping.

The streets were very full that day, but we got on pretty well as far as the bottom of Cheapside where there was a block for three or four minutes. The young man put his head out and said anxiously: 'I think I had better get out and walk; I shall never get there if this goes on.'

'I'll do all that can be done, sir,' said Jerry. 'I think we shall be in time; this block-up cannot last much longer, and your luggage is very heavy for you to carry, sir.'

Just then the cart in front of us began to move on, and then we had a good turn. In and out, in and out we went, as fast as horseflesh could do it, and for a wonder, we had a good clear time on London Bridge, for there was a whole train of cabs and carriages all going our way at a quick trot—perhaps wanting to catch that very train. At any rate, with many others, we whirled into the station just as the great clock pointed to eight minutes to twelve.

'Thank God! we are in time,' said the young man; 'and thank you, too, my friend, and your good horse. You have saved me more than money can ever pay for; take this extra half-crown.'

'No, sir, no, thank you all the same. So glad we hit the time, sir; but don't stay now, sir, the bell is ringing. Here, porter! take this gentleman's luggage—Dover line—twelve o'clock train—that's it;' and without waiting for another word, Jerry wheeled me round to make room for other cabs that were dashing up at the last minute, and drew up on one side till the crush was past.

'So glad!' he said, 'so glad! poor young fellow! I wonder what it was that made him so anxious.'

Jerry often talked to himself quite loud enough for me to hear when we were not moving.

On Jerry's return to the rank there was a good deal of laughing and chaffing at him for driving hard to the train for an extra fare, as they said, all against his principles; and they wanted to know how much he had pocketed.

'A good deal more than I generally get,' said he, nodding

slyly; 'what he gave me will keep me in little comforts for several days.'

'Gammon!' said one.

'He's a humbug,' said another, 'preaching to us, and then doing the same himself.'

'Look here, mates,' said Jerry. 'The gentleman offered me half a crown extra, but I didn't take it; 'twas quite pay enough for me to see how glad he was to catch that train; and if Jack and I choose to have a quick run now and then to please ourselves, that's our business and not yours.'

'Well,' said Larry, '*you'll* never be a rich man.'

'Most likely not,' said Jerry, 'but I don't know that I shall be the less happy for that. I have heard the commandments read a great many times, and I never noticed that any of them said, "Thou shalt be rich"; and there are a good many curious things said in the New Testament about rich men that, I think, would make me feel rather queer if I was one of them.'

'If you ever do get rich,' said Governor Grant, looking over his shoulder across the top of his cab, 'you'll deserve it, Jerry, and you won't find a curse come with your wealth. As for you, Larry, you'll die poor, you spend too much in whipcord.'

'Well,' said Larry, 'what is a fellow to do if his horse won't go without it?'

'You never take the trouble to see if he will go without it; your whip is always going as if you had the St. Vitus's dance in your arm; and if it does not wear you out, it wears your horse out. You know you are always changing your horses, and why? because you never give them any peace or encouragement.'

'Well, I have not had good luck,' said Larry, 'that's where it is.'

'And you never will,' said the Governor. 'Good Luck is rather particular with whom she rides, and mostly prefers those who have common sense and a good heart; at least, that is my experience.'

Governor Grant turned round again to his newspaper, and the other men went to their cabs.

CHAPTER THIRTY-SIX

THE SUNDAY CAB

ONE morning, as Jerry had just put me into the shafts and was fastening the traces, a gentleman walked into the yard. 'Your servant, sir,' said Jerry.

'Good-morning, Mr. Barker,' said the gentleman. 'I should be glad to make some arrangement with you for taking Mrs. Briggs regularly to church on Sunday mornings. We go to the New Church now, and that is rather farther than she can walk.'

'Thank you, sir,' said Jerry, 'but I have only taken out a six days' licence,* and therefore I could not take a fare on a Sunday, it would not be legal.'

'Oh!' said the other, 'I did not know yours was a six days' cab; but of course it would be very easy to alter your licence. I would see that you did not lose by it; the fact is, Mrs. Briggs very much prefers you to drive her.'

'I should be glad to oblige the lady, sir, but I had a seven days' licence once, and the work was too hard for me and too hard for my horses. Year in and year out, not a day's rest, never a Sunday with my wife and children, and never able to go to a place of worship, which I had always been used to do before I took to the driving-box; so for the last five years I have taken only a six days' licence, and I find it better all the way round.'

'Well, of course,' replied Mr. Briggs, 'it is very proper that every person should have rest and be able to go to church on Sundays, but I should have thought you would not have minded such a short distance for the horse, and only once a day; you would have all the afternoon and evening for yourself, and we are very good customers, you know.'

* Some years since the annual charge for a cab licence was very much reduced, and the difference between the six and seven days cabs was abolished.

'Yes, sir, that is true, and I'm grateful for all favours, I am sure, and anything that I could do to oblige you or the lady, I should be proud and happy to do; but I can't give up my Sundays, sir, indeed I can't. I read that God made man, and He made horses and all the other beasts; and as soon as He made them, He made a day of rest, and bade that all should rest one day in seven. I think sir, He must have known what was good for them, and I am sure it is good for me. I am stronger and healthier all together now that I have a day of rest; the horses are fresh too, and do not wear up nearly so fast. The six-day drivers all tell me the same, and I have laid more money in the Savings' Bank than ever I did before; and as for my wife and children, sir—why, heart alive! they would not go back to the seven days' work for all they could get by it.'

'Oh, very well,' said the gentleman. 'Don't trouble yourself, Mr. Barker, any further; I will inquire somewhere else;' and he walked away.

'Well,' says Jerry to me, 'we can't help it, Jack, old boy, we must have our Sundays.'

Three weeks had passed away after this conversation, and no order had come from Mrs. Briggs; so there was nothing but taking jobs from the stand. Jerry took it to heart a good deal, for of course the work was harder for horse and man. But Polly would always cheer him up and say, 'Never mind, father, never mind—

> *Do your best,*
> *And leave the rest,*
> *'Twill all come right*
> *Some day or night.'*

It soon became known that Jerry had lost his best customer, and for what reason; most of the men said he was a fool, but two or three took his part.

'If working men don't stick to their Sunday,' said Truman, 'they'll soon have none left; it is every man's right, and every beast's right. By God's law we have a day of rest, and by the law of England we have a day of rest, and I say we ought to hold to the rights these laws give us, and keep them for our children.'

'All very well for you religious chaps to talk so,' said Larry, 'but I'll turn a shilling when I can. I don't believe in religion, for I don't see that your religious people are any better than the rest.'

'If they are not better,' put in Jerry, 'it is because they are not religious. You might as well say that our country's laws are not good because some people break them. If a man gives way to temper, and speaks evil of his neighbour, and does not pay his debts, he is *not* religious; I don't care how much he goes to church. If some men are shams and humbugs, that does not make religion untrue. Real religion is the best and the truest thing in the world, and the only thing that can make a man really happy, or make the world any better.'

'If religion was good for anything,' said Jones, 'it would prevent your religious people from making us work on Sundays, as you know many of them do, and that's why I say religion is nothing but a sham—why, if it was not for the church-and-chapel-goers it would be hardly worth while our coming out on a Sunday; but they have their privileges, as they call them, and I go without. I shall expect them to answer for my soul, if I can't get a chance of saving it.'

Several of the men applauded this, till Jerry said:—

'That may sound well enough, but it won't do; every man must look after his own soul; you can't lay it down at another man's door like a foundling, and expect him to take care of it; and don't you see, if you are always sitting on your box, waiting for a fare, they will say, "If we don't take him, some one else will, and he does not look for any Sunday." Of course they don't go to the bottom of it, or they would see if they never came for a cab, it would be no use your standing there; but people don't always like to go to the bottom of things; it may not be convenient to do it: but if you Sunday drivers would all strike for a day of rest, the thing would be done.'

'And what would all the good people do if they could not get to their favourite preachers?' said Larry.

''Tis not for me to lay down plans for other people,' said

Jerry, 'but if they can't walk so far, they can go to what is nearer; and if it should rain they can put on their mackintoshes as they do on a weekday. If a thing is right, it *can* be done, and if it is wrong, it *can be done without*; and a good man will find a way; and that is as true for us cabmen as it is for the church-goers.'

CHAPTER THIRTY-SEVEN

THE GOLDEN RULE

Two or three weeks after this, as we came into the yard rather late in the evening, Polly came running across the road with the lantern (she always brought it to him if it was not very wet).

'It has all come right, Jerry; Mrs. Briggs sent her servant this afternoon to ask you to take her out to-morrow at eleven o'clock. I said, yes, I thought you could, but we supposed she employed some one else now.

' "Well," says he, "the real fact is, master was put out because Mr. Barker refused to come out on Sundays, and he has been trying other cabs, but there's something wrong with them all; some drive too fast, and some too slow; and the mistress says there is not a cab so nice and clean as yours; so nothing will suit her but Mr. Barker's cab again." '

Polly was almost out of breath, and Jerry broke out into a merry laugh:—

> '*All will come right*
> *Some day or night.*

You were right, my dear; you generally are. Run in and get the supper, and I'll have Jack's harness off and make him snug and happy in no time.'

After this Mrs. Briggs wanted Jerry's cab quite as often as before; never, however, on a Sunday. But there came a day when we had Sunday work, and this was how it happened.

We had all come home on the Saturday night very tired, and very glad to think that the next day would be all rest; but it was not to be so.

On Sunday morning Jerry was cleaning me in the yard, when Polly stepped up to him, looking very full of something.

'What is it?' said Jerry.

'Well, my dear,' she said, 'poor Dinah Brown has just received a letter to say that her mother is dangerously ill, and that she must go directly if she wishes to see her alive. The place is more than ten miles away from here, right out in the country; and she says if she took the train she should still have four miles to walk; and so weak as she is, and the baby only four weeks old, of course that would be impossible. She wants to know if you would take her in your cab, and she promises to to pay you faithfully as soon as she can get the money.'

'Tut, tut, we'll see about that. It was not the money I was thinking about, but of losing our Sunday; the horses are tired, and I am tired too—that's where it pinches.'

'It pinches all round, for that matter,' said Polly, 'for it's only half Sunday without you. But you know we should do to other people as we would like them to do to us. I know very well what I should like if my mother was dying; and Jerry, dear, I am sure it won't break the Sabbath; for if pulling a poor beast or donkey out of a pit would not spoil the Sabbath, I am quite sure taking poor Dinah would not.'

'Why, Polly, you are as good as the minister; so, as I've had my Sunday morning sermon early to-day, you may go and tell Dinah that I'll be ready for her as the clock strikes ten. But stop—just step round to Butcher Braydon's, with my compliments, and ask him if he would lend me his light trap; I know he never uses it on the Sunday, and it would make a wonderful difference to the horse.'

Away she went, and soon returned, saying that he could have the trap and welcome.

'All right,' said he; 'now put me up a bit of bread and cheese, and I'll be back in the afternoon as soon as I can.'

'And I'll have the meat pie ready for an early tea instead of for dinner,' said Polly. And away she went, whilst he made his preparations to the tune of 'Polly, the woman and no mistake,' of which tune he was very fond.

I was selected for the journey, and at ten o'clock we started in a light, high-wheeled gig, which ran so easily that, after the four-wheeled cab, it seemed like nothing.

It was a fine May day, and soon as we were out of the town the sweet air, the smell of the fresh grass, and the soft country roads were as pleasant as they used to be in the old times, and I soon began to feel quite fresh.

Dinah's family lived in a small farmhouse up a green lane, close by a meadow with some fine shady trees; there were two cows feeding in it. A young man asked Jerry to bring his trap into the meadow, and he would tie me up in the cowshed; he wished he had a better stable to offer.

'If your cows would not be offended,' said Jerry, 'there is nothing my horse would like so well as to have an hour or two in your beautiful meadow. He's quiet, and it would be a rare treat for him.'

'Put him there and welcome,' said the young man. 'The best we have is at your service for your kindness to my sister; we shall be having some dinner in an hour, and I hope you'll come in, though with mother so ill we are all out of sorts in the house.'

Jerry thanked him kindly, but said as he had some dinner with him, there was nothing he should like so well as walking about in the meadow.

When my harness was taken off, I did not know what I should do first—roll over on my back, lie down and rest, or have a gallop across the meadow out of sheer spirits at being free; so I did all by turns. Jerry seemed to be quite as happy as I was. He sat down by a bank under a shady tree, and listened to the birds; then he sang to himself, and read out of the little brown book he is so fond of; next he wandered round the meadow and down by a little brook, where he picked the flowers and the hawthorn, and tied them up with long sprays of ivy; lastly he gave me a good feed of oats which he had brought with him. But the time seemed all too short—I had not been in a field since I left poor Ginger at Earlshall.

We came home at a gentle pace, and Jerry's first words were

as we came into the yard, 'Well, Polly, I have not lost my
Sunday after all, for the birds were singing hymns in every
bush, and I joined in the service; and as for Jack, he was like a
young colt.'

When he handed Dolly the flowers she jumped for joy.

CHAPTER THIRTY-EIGHT

DOLLY AND A REAL GENTLEMAN

THE winter came in early with a great deal of cold and wet.
There was snow, sleet, or rain almost every day for weeks,
changing only to keen, driving winds or sharp frosts. We all felt
it very much. When it is a dry cold, a couple of good thick
rugs will keep the warmth in us; but when it is a soaking rain,
they soon get wet through and are no good. Some of the drivers
had a waterproof cover to throw over us; this was a fine thing.

But some of the men were so poor that they could not protect
either themselves or their horses, and many of them suffered
very much that winter. When we horses had worked half the
day we went to our dry stables, and could rest; whilst the
drivers had to sit on their boxes, sometimes staying out as late
as one or two o'clock in the morning if they had to wait for a
party.

When the streets were slippery with frost or snow, that was
the worst of all for us horses; one mile of such travelling, with
a weight to draw and no firm footing, would take more out of
us than four on a good road. Every nerve and muscle of our
body is on the strain to keep our balance; and added to this, the
fear of falling is more exhausting than anything else. If the
roads are very bad indeed, our shoes are roughed, but this
makes us feel nervous at first.

When the weather was very bad, many of the men would go
and sit in the tavern close by, and get some one to watch for
them; but they often lost a fare in this way, and could not, as
Jerry said, be there without spending money.

He never went to the 'Rising Sun.' There was a coffee-shop near where he now and then went; or he bought off an old man who came to our rank with tins of hot coffee and pies. It was Jerry's opinion that spirits and beer made a man colder afterwards, and that dry clothes, good food, cheerfulness, and a comfortable wife at home were the best things to keep a cabman warm.

Polly always supplied him with something to eat when he could not get home, and sometimes he would see little Dolly peeping from the corner of the street, to make sure if 'Father' was on the stand. If she saw him, she would run off at full speed and soon come back with something in a tin or basket—some hot soup or pudding that Polly had ready.

It was wonderful how such a little thing could get safely across the street, often thronged with horses and carriages; but she was a brave little maid; and felt it quite an honour to bring 'Father's first course,' as he called it. She was a general favourite on the stand, and there was not a man who would not have seen her safely across the street, if Jerry had not been able to do so.

One cold, windy day, Dolly had brought Jerry a basin of something hot, and was standing by him whilst he ate it. He had scarcely begun when a gentleman walking towards us very quickly held up his umbrella. Jerry touched his hat in return, gave the basin to Dolly, and was taking off my cloth, when the gentleman, hastening up, cried out, 'No, no, finish your soup, my friend; I have not much time to spare, but I can wait till you have done, and have set your little girl safely on the pavement.' So saying, he seated himself in the cab. Jerry thanked him kindly, and came back to Dolly.

'There, Dolly, that's a gentleman; that's a real gentleman, Dolly; he has both time and thought for the comfort of a poor cabman and a little girl.'

Jerry finished his soup, saw the child safely across the road, and then took his orders to drive to Clapham Rise. Several times after this the same gentleman took our cab. I think he was very fond of dogs and horses, for whenever we took him to his own door, two or three dogs would come bounding out to meet him. Sometimes he came round and patted me, saying in his quiet, pleasant way, 'This horse has a good master, and he deserves it.'

It was a very rare thing for any one to notice the horse that had been working for him. I have known ladies do it now and then, and this gentleman and one or two others have given me a pat and a kind word; but ninety-nine out of a hundred would as soon think of patting the steam-engine that drew the train.

This gentleman was not young, and there was a forward stoop in his shoulders, as if he was always going at something. His lips were thin and close shut, though they had a very pleasant smile; his eye was keen, and there was something in his jaw and the motion of his head that made one think he was very determined in anything he set about doing. His voice was pleasant and kind; any horse would trust that voice, though it was just as decided as everything else about him.

One day, he and another gentleman took our cab. They stopped at a shop in R—— Street, and whilst his friend went in he stood at the door. A little ahead of us, on the other side of the street, a cart with two very fine horses was standing before some wine-vaults; the carter was not with them, and I cannot tell how long they had been standing but they seemed to think they had waited long enough, and began to move off. Before they had gone many paces, the carter came running out and caught them. He seemed furious at their having moved, and with whip and rein punished them brutally, even beating them about the head.

Our gentleman saw it all, and stepping quickly across the street, said in a decided voice, 'If you don't stop that directly, I'll have you summoned for leaving your horses and for brutal conduct.'

The man, who had clearly been drinking, poured forth some abusive language, but he left off knocking the horses about, and taking the reins, got into his cart. Meanwhile our friend had quietly taken a note book from his pocket, and looking at the name and address painted on the cart, he wrote something down.

'What do you want with that?' growled the carter, as he

cracked his whip and was moving on. A nod and a grim smile was the only answer he got.

On returning to the cab, our friend was joined by his companion, who said laughingly, 'I should have thought, Wright, you had enough business of your own to look after without troubling yourself about other people's horses and servants.'

Our friend stood still for a moment, and throwing his head a little back, said, 'Do you know why this world is as bad as it is?'

'No,' said the other.

'Then I'll tell you. It is because people think *only* about their own business, and won't trouble themselves to stand up for the oppressed, nor bring the wrongdoer to light. I never see a wicked thing like this without doing what I can, and many a master has thanked me for letting him know how his horses have been used.'

'I wish there were more gentlemen like you, sir,' said Jerry, 'for they are wanted badly enough in this city.'

After this we continued our journey, and as they got out of the cab our friend was saying, 'My doctrine is this, that if we see cruelty or wrong that we have the power to stop, and yet do nothing, we make ourselves sharers in the guilt.'

CHAPTER THIRTY-NINE

SEEDY SAM

I SHOULD say that for a cab-horse I was very well off indeed; my driver was my owner, and it was to his interest to treat me well and not to overwork me, even had he not been so good a man as he was; but there were a great many horses which belonged to the large cab-owners, who let them out to their drivers for so much money a day. As the horses did not belong to these men, the only thing they thought of was how to get their money out of the horses, first to pay their master, and then to provide their own living; and a dreadful time some of these horses had of it. Of course I understood but little, but it was often talked over on the stand, and the Governor, who was a kind-hearted man and fond of horses, would sometimes speak his mind if a horse came in very much jaded or ill-used.

One day a shabby, miserable-looking driver, who went by the name of 'Seedy Sam,' brought in his horse looking dreadfully beat, and the Governor said, 'You and your horse look more fit for the police-station than for this rank.'

The man flung his tattered rug over the horse, turned full round upon the Governor, and said, in a voice that sounded almost desperate:—

'If the police have any business with the matter, it ought to be the masters who charge us so much, or with the fares that are fixed so low. If a man has to pay eighteen shillings a day for the use of a cab and two horses, as many of us have to do in the season, and must make that up before he earns a penny for himself—I say, 'tis more than hard work. Nine shillings a day to get out of each horse before you begin to get your own living! You know that's true, and if the horses don't work we must starve.

'My children and I have known what that is before now. I've six of 'em, and only one earns anything. I am on the stand fourteen or sixteen hours a day, and I haven't had a Sunday these ten or twelve weeks. You know, Skinner never gives a day if he can help it; and if I don't work hard, tell me who does! I want a warm coat and a mackintosh, but with so many to feed, how can a man get it? I had to pledge my clock a week ago to pay Skinner, and I shall never see it again.'

Some of the other drivers stood round nodding their heads, and saying he was right. The man went on: 'You that have your own horses and cabs, or drive for good masters, have a chance of getting on, and a chance of doing right; I haven't. Within the four-mile radius we can't charge more than sixpence a mile after the first mile.

'This very morning I had to go a clear six miles and took only three shillings. I could not get a return fare, and had to come half the way back; there's twelve miles for the horse and three shillings for me.

'After that I had a three-mile fare, and there were bags and boxes enough to have brought in a good many tuppences if they had been put outside. But you know how people do—all that could be piled up inside on the front seat were put in, and three heavy boxes went on the top—that was.sixpence, and the fare one and sixpence. Then I got a return for a shilling; now that makes eighteen miles for the horse and six shillings for me. There's three shillings still for that horse to earn, and nine shillings for the afternoon horse before I touch a penny.

'Of course it is not always as bad as that, but you know it often is; and I say 'tis mockery to tell a man that he must not overwork his horse, for when a beast is downright tired, there's nothing but the whip that will keep his legs going—you can't help yourself. You must put your wife and children before the horse; the masters must look to that, we can't. I don't ill-use my horse for the sake of doing so; none of you can say I do.

'There's wrong lying somewhere—never a day's rest, never a quiet hour with the wife and children. I often feel like an old man, though I'm only forty-five. You know how quick some of the gentry are to suspect us of cheating and overcharging. Why, they stand with their purses in their hands, counting the fare over to a penny, and looking at us as if we were pickpockets. I wish some of 'em had got to sit on my box sixteen hours a a day, and had to get a living out of it and eighteen shillings besides, and to do it in all weathers; they would not then be so uncommonly particular never to give us a sixpence over, nor would they then cram all the luggage inside. Of course, some of 'em tip us pretty handsomely now and then, or else we could not live; but we can't *depend* upon that.'

The men who stood round much approved of this speech. One of them said, 'It is desperate hard, and if a man sometimes does what is wrong, it is no wonder; and if he gets a dram too much, who's to blow him up?'

Jerry had taken no part in this conversation, but I never saw his face look so sad before. The Governor had stood with both his hands in his pockets; now he took his handkerchief out of his hat, and wiped his forehead.

'You've beaten me, Sam,' he said, 'for it's all true, and I

won't cast it up against you any more about the police. It was the look in that horse's eye that came over me. It is hard lines for both man and beast, and who's to mend it, I don't know; but anyway you might tell the poor beast that you were sorry to take it out of him in that way. Sometimes a kind word is all we can give 'em, poor brutes, and 'tis wonderful what they understand.'

A few mornings after this talk a new man came on the stand with Sam's cab.

'Halloo!' said one, 'what's up with Seedy Sam?'

'He's ill in bed,' said the man; 'he was taken ill last night in the yard, and could scarcely crawl home. His wife sent a boy this morning to say his father was in a high fever and could not get out so I'm here instead.'

The next morning the same man came again.

'How is Sam?' inquired the Governor.

'He's gone,' said the man.

'What! gone? You don't mean to say he's dead?'

'Just snuffed out,' said the other; 'he died at four o'clock this morning. All yesterday he was raving—raving about Skinner and about having no Sundays. "I never had a Sunday's rest," these were his last words.'

No one spoke for a while, and then the Governor said, 'I tell you what, mates, this is a warning to us all.'

CHAPTER FORTY

POOR GINGER

ONE day, whilst our cab and many others were waiting outside one of the parks where a band was playing, a shabby old cab drove up beside ours. The horse was an old worn-out chestnut with an ill-kept coat, and with bones that showed plainly through it. The knees knuckled over, and the forelegs were very unsteady.

I had been eating some hay, and the wind rolling a little lock

of it that way, the poor creature put out her long, thin neck
and picked it up, and then turned round and looked about for
more. There was a hopeless look in the dull eye that I could not
help noticing; and then, as I was thinking where I had seen
that horse before, she looked full at me and said, 'Black Beauty,
is that you?'

It was Ginger! but how changed! The beautifully arched
and glossy neck was now straight, lank, and fallen in; the clean,
straight legs and delicate fetlocks were swollen; the joints were
grown out of shape with hard work; the face that was once so
full of spirit and life was now full of suffering; and I could tell
by the heaving of her sides and by her frequent cough how bad
her breath was.

Our drivers were standing together a little way off, so I sidled
up to her a step or two that we might have a little quiet talk.
It was a sad tale that she had to tell.

After a twelve-months' run off at Earlshall, she was considered to be fit for work again, and was sold to a gentleman.
For a little while she got on very well, but after a longer gallop
than usual, the old strain returned, and, after being rested and
doctored, she was again sold. In this way she changed hands
several times, but always getting lower down.

'And so at last,' said she, 'I was bought by a man who keeps
a number of cabs and horses, and lets them out. You look well
off, and I'm glad of it; but I cannot tell you what my life has
been. When they found out my weakness, they said I was not
worth what they gave for me, and that I must go into one of
the low cabs and just be used up; that is what they are doing—
whipping and working me, with never one thought of what I
suffer. They paid for me, and must get the money out of me,
they say. The man who hires me now pays a deal of money to
the dealer every day, and so he has to get it out of me first; and so
it goes on all the weeks round, with never a Sunday rest.'

I said, 'You used to stand up for yourself if you were ill-used.'

'Ah!' she said, 'I did once, but it's no use; men are stronger,
and if they are cruel and have no feeling, there is nothing that
we can do but just bear it—bear it on and on to the end. I wish
the end was come; I wish I was dead. I have seen dead horses

and I am sure they do not suffer pain; I hope I may drop down dead at my work, and not be sent off to the knacker's.'

I was very much troubled, and I put my nose up to hers, but I could say nothing to comfort her. I think she was pleased to see me, for she said, 'You are the only friend I ever had.'

Just then her driver came up, and with a tug at her mouth backed her out of the line and drove off, leaving me very sad indeed.

A short time after this a cart with a dead horse in it passed our cab-stand. The head hung out of the cart tail, the lifeless tongue was slowly dropping blood; and the sunken eyes!—but I can't speak of them, the sight was too dreadful. It was a chestnut horse with a long, thin neck. I saw a white streak down the forehead. I believe it was Ginger; I hoped it was, for then her troubles would be over. Oh! if men were more merciful they would shoot us before we come to such misery.

CHAPTER FORTY-ONE

THE BUTCHER

I SAW a great deal of trouble amongst the horses in London, much of which might have been prevented by a little common sense. We horses do not mind hard work if we are treated reasonably; and I am sure there are many driven by quite poor men who have a happier life than I had when, with my silver-mounted harness, I used to go in the Countess of W——'s carriage.

It often went to my heart to see how badly the little ponies were used—straining along with heavy loads, or staggering under heavy blows from some low, cruel boy. Once I saw a little grey pony with a thick mane and a pretty head, and so much like Merrylegs that if I had not been in harness I should have neighed to him. He was doing his best to pull a heavy cart, while a strong rough boy was cutting him under the belly with his whip, and chucking cruelly at his little mouth.

Could it be Merrylegs? It was just like him; but then Mr.
Blomefield was never to sell him, and I do not think he would
have done so. Yet this may have been quite as good a little
fellow, and have had as happy a place when he was young.

I often noticed the great speed at which butchers' horses
were made to go, though I did not know why they were driven
so fast till one day when we had to wait some time in St. John's
Wood. There was a butcher's shop next door, and as we were
standing a butcher's cart came dashing up at a great pace. The
horse was hot and much exhausted; he hung his head down,
while his heaving sides and trembling legs showed how hard
he had been driven. The lad jumped out of the cart and was
getting the basket when the master came out of the shop much
displeased. After looking at the horse, he turned angrily to the
lad.

'How many times shall I tell you not to drive in this way?
You ruined the last horse and broke his wind, and you are going
to ruin this in the same way?. If you were not my own son, I
would dismiss you on the spot; it is a disgrace to have a horse
brought to the shop in such a condition. You are liable to be
taken up by the police for furious driving, and if you are, you
need not look to me for bail, for I have spoken to you till I'm
tired; you must look out for yourself.'

During this speech the boy had stood by, sullen and dogged;
but when his father ceased, he broke out angrily, 'It wasn't my
fault, and I won't take the blame: I am only going by orders
all the time.

'You always say, "Now be quick; now look sharp!" And
when I go to the houses, one person wants a leg of mutton for
an early dinner, and I must be back with it in a quarter of an
hour; another has forgotten to order the beef, and I must go
and fetch it and be back in no time or the mistress will scold;
the third says they have company coming unexpectedly and must
have some chops sent up directly; and the lady at No. 4 in the
Crescent *never* orders her dinner till the meat comes in for
lunch—it's nothing but hurry, hurry, all the time. If the gentry
would think of what they want, and order their meat the day
before, there need not be this blow up!'

'I wish to goodness they would,' said the butcher; ''twould save me a wonderful deal of harass, and I could suit my customers much better if I knew before-hand. But there—what's the use of talking? Whoever thinks of a butcher's convenience, or a butcher's horse? Now then, take him in, and look to him well. Mind, he does not go out again to-day, and if anything else is wanted, you must carry it yourself in the basket.' With that he went in and the horse was led away.

But all the boys are not cruel. I have seen some as fond of their pony or donkey as if it had been a favourite dog; and the little creatures have worked away as cheerfully and willingly for their young drivers as I work for Jerry. It may be hard work sometimes, but a friends' hand and voice make it easy.

There was a young coster-boy who came up our street with greens and potatoes. He had an old pony, not very handsome, but the most cheerful and plucky little thing I ever saw; and to see how fond those two were of each other was a treat. The pony followed his master like a dog; and when the boy got into his cart, the pony would trot off without a whip or a word and rattle down the street as merrily as if he had come out of the Queen's stables. Jerry liked the boy and called him 'Prince Charlie,' for he said he would make a king of drivers some day.

There was an old man too, who used to come up our street with a little coal cart. He wore a coal-heaver's hat, and looked rough and black. He and his old horse used to plod together along the street like two good partners who understood each other. The horse would stop of his own accord at the doors where they took coal of him. He used to keep one ear bent towards his master. The old man's cry could be heard up the street long before he came near. I never knew what he said, but the children called him 'Old Ba-a-ar Hoo,' for it sounded like that. Polly bought her coal of him, and was very friendly; and Jerry said it was a comfort to think how happy an old horse may be in a poor place.

CHAPTER FORTY-TWO

THE ELECTION

As we came into the yard one afternoon, Polly came out, 'Jerry! I've had Mr. B—— here asking about your vote, and he wants to hire your cab for the election; he will call for an answer.'

'Well, Polly, you may say that my cab will be otherwise engaged; I should not like to have it pasted over with their great bills, and as to make Jack and Captain race about to the public-houses to bring up half-drunken voters, why, I think 'twould be an insult to the horses. No, I shan't do it.'

'I suppose you'll vote for the gentleman? He said he was of your politics.'

'So he is in some things, but I shall not vote for him, Polly; you know what his trade is?'

'Yes.'

'Well, a man who gets rich by that trade may be all very well in some ways, but he is blind to what working men want; I could not in my conscience send him up to make the laws. I daresay they'll be angry, but every man must do what he thinks to be the best for his country.'

On the morning before the election Jerry was putting me into the shafts, when Dolly came into the yard sobbing and crying, with her little blue frock and white pinafore spattered all over with mud.

'Why, Dolly, what is the matter?'

'Those naughty boys,' she sobbed, 'have thrown the dirt all over me, and called me a little raga—raga—'

'They called her a little blue ragamuffin, father,' said Harry, who ran in looking very angry; 'but I have given it to them; they won't insult my sister again. I have given them a thrashing they will remember; a set of cowardly, rascally, orange blackguards!'

Jerry kissed the child and said, 'Run in to mother, my pet,

and tell her I think you had better stay at home to-day and help
her.'

Then, turning gravely to Harry:—

'My boy, I hope you will always defend your sister, and give
anybody who insults her a good thrashing— that is as it should
be; but mind, I won't have any election blackguarding on my
premises. There are as many blue blackguards as there are
orange, and as many white as there are purple, or any other
colour, and I won't have any of my family mixed up with it.
Even women and children are ready to quarrel for the sake of
a colour, and not one in ten of them know what it is about.'

'Why, father, I thought blue was for Liberty.'

'My boy, Liberty does not come from colours, they only
show party, and all the liberty you can get out of them is liberty
to get drunk at other peoples' expense, liberty to ride to the
poll in a dirty old cab, liberty to abuse any one that does not
wear your colour, and to shout yourself hoarse at what you
only half-understand—that's your liberty!'

'Oh, father, you are laughing.'

'No, Harry, I am serious, and I am ashamed to see how men
go on that ought to know better. An election is a very serious
thing; at least, it ought to be, and every man ought to vote
according to his conscience, and let his neighbour do the same.'

CHAPTER FORTY-THREE

A FRIEND IN NEED

It was the day of the election. Jerry would not let his cab to
either party, but there was no lack of work for us.

First came a stout, puffy gentleman with a carpet-bag, who
wanted to go to the Bishopsgate Station; then we were called
by a party who wished to be taken to the Regent's Park; and
next we were wanted in a side street, where a timid, anxious
old lady was waiting to be taken to the Bank. There we had to
stop to take her back again; and just as we had set her down,

a red-faced gentleman with a handful of papers came running up, out of breath; and before Jerry could get down, he had opened the door, popped himself in, and called out, 'Bow Street Police Station, quick!' So off we went with him; and when after another turn or two we came back, there was no other cab on the stand. Jerry put on my nose-bag, for, as he said, 'We must eat when we can on such days as these; so munch away, Jack, and make the best of your time, old boy.'

I found I had a good feed of crushed oats, wetted with a little bran; this would be a treat any day, but was specially refreshing now. Jerry was so thoughtful and kind—what horse would not do his best for such a master? Then he took out one of Polly's meat pies, and standing near me, he began to eat it.

The streets were very full, and the cabs with the candidates' colours on them were dashing about through the crowd as if life and limb were of no consequence. We saw two people knocked down that day, and one was a woman. The horses were having a bad time of it, poor things! but the voters inside thought nothing of that, for many of them were half drunk, hurrahing out of the cab windows if their own party came by. It was the first election I had seen, and I don't want to be in another, though I have heard things are better now.

Jerry and I had not eaten many mouthfuls before a poor young woman, carrying a heavy child, came along the street. She was looking this way and that way, and seemed quite bewildered. Presently she made her way up to Jerry and asked if he could tell her the way to St. Thomas's Hospital, and how far it was to get there. She had come from the country that morning in a market cart, and did not know it was the election. She was quite a stranger in London, but had got an order for the hospital for her little boy, who was crying with a feeble, pining cry.

'Poor little fellow!' she said, 'he suffers a deal of pain. He is four years old, and can't walk any more than a baby; but the doctor said if I could get him into the hospital, he might get well. Pray, sir, how far is it? and which way must I go?'

'Why missis,' said Jerry, 'you can't get there walking through crowds like this! Why, it is three miles away, and that child is heavy.'

'Yes, bless him, he is, but I am strong, thank God; and if I knew the way, I think I could get on somehow: please tell me the way.'

'You can't do it,' said Jerry; 'you might be knocked down and the child be run over. Now look here, just get into this cab, and I'll drive you safely to the hospital: don't you see the rain is coming on?'

'No, sir, no, I can't do that, thank you; I have only just money enough to get back with. Please tell me the way.'

'Look you here, missis,' said Jerry, 'I've got a wife and dear children at home, and I know a father's feelings. Now get into that cab and I'll take you there for nothing; I'd be ashamed of myself to let a woman and a sick child run a risk like that.'

'Heaven bless you!' said the woman, and she burst into tears.

'There, there, cheer up, my dear, I'll soon take you there. Come, let me put you inside.'

As Jerry went to open the door, two men with colours in their hats and button-holes ran up, calling out, 'Cab!'

'Engaged!' cried Jerry. But one of the men, pushing past the woman, sprang into the cab, followed by the other. Jerry looked as stern as a policeman: 'This cab is already engaged, gentlemen, by that lady.'

'Lady!' said one of them; 'oh! she can wait: our business is very important; besides, we were in first. It is our right, and we shall stay in.'

A droll smile came over Jerry's face as he shut the door upon them. 'All right, gentlemen; pray stay in as long as it suits you. I can wait while you rest yourselves;' and turning his back upon them, he walked up to the young woman, who was standing near me. 'They'll soon be gone,' he said, laughing; 'don't trouble yourself, my dear.'

And they soon were gone; for when they understood Jerry's dodge, they got out, calling him all sorts of bad names, and blustering about his number and getting a summons. After this little stoppage we were soon on our way to the hospital, going as much as possible through by-streets. Jerry rang the great bell, and helped the young woman out.

'Thank you a thousand times,' she said; 'I could never have got here alone.'

'You're kindly welcome, and I hope the dear child will soon be better.'

He watched her go in at the door, and he said to himself quietly, '"Inasmuch as ye have done it to one of the least of these."' Then he patted my neck; this was always his way when anything pleased him.

The rain was now coming down fast, and just as we were leaving the hospital the door opened again, and the porter called out, 'Cab!' We stopped, and a lady came down the steps. Jerry seemed to know her at once. She put back her veil, and said, 'Barker! Jeremiah Barker! is it you? I am very glad to find you here; you are just the friend I want, for it is very difficult to get a cab in this part of London to-day.'

'I shall be proud to serve you, ma'am; I am right glad I happened to be here. Where may I take you to, ma'am?'

'To the Paddington Station, and then if we are in good time, as I think we shall be, you shall tell me all about Mary and the children.'

We got to the station in good time, and being under shelter, the lady stood a good while talking to Jerry. I found she had been Polly's mistress, and after many inquiries about her, she said, 'How do you find the cab-work suits you in winter? I know Mary was rather anxious about you last year.'

'Yes, ma'am, she was; I had a bad cough that followed me up quite into the warm weather, and when I am kept out late she does worry herself a good deal. You see, ma'am, my work is at all hours and in all weathers, and that does try a man's constitution; but I am getting on pretty well, and I should feel quite lost if I had not horses to look after. I was brought up to it, and I am afraid I should not do as well at anything else.'

'Well, Barker,' she said, 'it would be a great pity that you should seriously risk your health in this work, not only for your own but for Mary's and the children's sake. There are many places where good drivers or good grooms are wanted; and if ever you think you ought to give up this cab-work, let me know.' Then sending some kind messages to Mary, she put something into his hand, saying, 'There are five shillings each for the two children; Mary will know how to spend it.'

Jerry thanked her and seemed much pleased; then, turning out of the station, we at last reached home; I, at least, was tired.

CHAPTER FORTY-FOUR

OLD CAPTAIN AND HIS SUCCESSOR

CAPTAIN and I were great friends. He was a noble old fellow, and a very good companion. I never thought that he would have to leave his home and go down the hill, but his turn came; and this is how it happened. I was not there, but I heard all about it.

Jerry and he had taken a party to the great railway station over London bridge, and were coming back, somewhere between the bridge and the Monument, when Jerry saw a brewer's empty dray coming along, drawn by two powerful horses. The drayman was slashing his horses with his heavy whip. The dray was light, and they were going at a furious rate. The man had no control over them.

The street was full of traffic; one young girl was knocked down and run over, and the next moment the dray dashed up against our cab; both the wheels were torn off, and the cab was thrown over. Captain was dragged down, the shafts splintered, and one of them ran into his side. Jerry, too, was thrown, but was only bruised. Nobody could tell how he escaped; he always said 'twas a miracle.

When poor Captain was got up, he was found to be very much cut and knocked about. Jerry led him home gently, and a sad sight it was to see the blood soaking into his white coat and dropping from his side and shoulder. The drayman being proved to be very drunk, was fined, and the brewer had to pay damages to our master; but there was no one to pay damages to poor Captain.

At first Captain seemed to do well, but he was a very old horse, and it was only his wonderful constitution and Jerry's care that had kept him up at the cab-work so long; now he broke down very much. The farrier said he might mend up enough to sell for a few pounds, but Jerry said, No! a few pounds got by selling a good old servant into hard work and misery would canker all the rest of his money. He thought the kindest thing he could do for the fine old fellow would be to put a sure bullet through his heart, and then he would never suffer more; for he did not know where to find him a kind master for the rest of his days.

The day after this was decided Harry took me to the forge for some new shoes. When I returned Captain was gone. The family and I all felt it very much.

Jerry had now to look out for another horse, and he soon heard of one through an acquaintance who was under-groom in a nobleman's stables. He was a valuable young horse, but he had run away, smashed into another carriage, flung his lordship out, and so cut and blemished himself that he was no longer fit for a gentleman's stables, and the coachman had orders to look round and sell him as well as he could.

'I can do with high spirits,' said Jerry, 'if a horse is not vicious or hard-mouthed.'

'There is not a bit of vice in him,' said the man; 'his mouth is very tender, and I think myself that was the cause of the accident. You see, he had just been clipped, and the weather was bad, and he had not had exercise enough, and when he did go out he was as full of spring as a balloon. Our governor (the coachman, I mean) had him harnessed in as tight and strong as he could, with the martingale, and the bearing rein, a very sharp curb, and the reins, put in at the bottom bar; it is my belief that it made the horse mad, being tender in the mouth and so full of spirit.'

'Likely enough; I'll come and see him,' said Jerry.

The next day, Hotspur—that was his name—came home; he was a fine brown horse, without a white hair in him, as tall as

Captain, with a very handsome head, and only five years old. I gave him a friendly greeting by way of good-fellowship, but did not ask him any questions. The first night he was very restless; instead of lying down, he kept jerking his halter rope up and down through the ring, and knocking the block about against the manger so that I could not sleep. However, the next day, after five or six hours in the cab, he came in quiet and sensible. Jerry patted and talked to him a good deal, and very soon they understood each other, and Jerry said that with an easy bit and plenty of work he would be as gentle as a lamb, and that it was an ill wind that blew nobody good, for if his lordship had lost a hundred-guinea favourite, the cabman had gained a good horse with all his strength in him.

Hotspur thought it a great come-down to be a cab-horse, and was disgusted at standing in the rank, but he confessed to me at the end of the week that an easy mouth and a free head made up for a great deal, and, after all, the work was not so degrading as having one's head and tail fastened to each other at the saddle. In fact, he settled in well, and Jerry liked him very much.

CHAPTER FORTY-FIVE

JERRY'S NEW YEAR

CHRISTMAS and the New Year are very merry times for some people; but for cabmen and cabmen's horses these times are no holiday, though they may be a harvest. There are so many parties, balls, and places of amusement open that the work is hard and often late. Sometimes driver and horse, shivering with cold, have to wait for hours in the rain or frost, whilst the merry people within are dancing to the music. I wonder if the beautiful ladies ever think of the weary cabman waiting on his box, and of his patient beast standing till his legs get stiff with cold!

I had now most of the evening work as I was well accustomed to standing, and Jerry was also more afraid of Hotspur, the new horse, taking cold. We had a great deal of late work in the

Christmas week, and Jerry's cough was bad, but, however late we were, Polly sat up for him, and, looking anxious and troubled, she came out with the lantern to meet him.

On the evening of the New Year we had to take two gentlemen to a house in one of the West End squares. We set them down at nine o'clock, and were told to come again at eleven. 'But,' said one of them, 'as it is a card party, you may have to wait a few minutes, but don't be late.'

As the clock struck eleven we were at the door, for Jerry was always punctual. The clock chimed the quarters—one, two, three, and then struck twelve; but the door did not open.

The wind had been very changeable, with squalls of rain during the day, but now it came on sharp, driving sleet, which seemed to come all the way round one; it was very cold, and there was no shelter. Jerry got off his box and came and pulled one of my cloths a little more over my neck; then, stamping his feet, he took a turn or two up and down; then he began to beat his arms, but that set him on coughing; so he opened the cab door and sat at the bottom with his feet on the pavement, and was thus a little sheltered. Still the clock chimed the quarters, but no one came. At half-past twelve he rang the bell, and asked the servant if he would be wanted that night.

'Oh, yes! you'll be wanted safe enough,' said the man; 'you must not go, it will soon be over.' And again Jerry sat down, but his voice was so hoarse I could hardly hear him.

At a quarter past one the door opened, and the two gentlemen came out; they got into the cab without a word, and told Jerry where to drive; it was nearly two miles away. My legs were numb with cold, and I thought I should have stumbled. When the men got out they never said they were sorry to have kept us waiting so long, but were angry at the charge. However, as Jerry never charged more than was his due, he never took less, and so they had to pay for the two hours and a quarter of waiting; but it was hard-earned money to Jerry.

At last we got home. He could hardly speak, and his cough was dreadful. Polly asked no questions, but opened the door and held the lantern for him.

'Can't I do something?' she said.

'Yes; get Jack something warm, and then boil me some gruel.'

This was said in a hoarse whisper. He could hardly get his breath, but he gave me a rub down as usual, and even went up into the hayloft for an extra bundle of straw for my bed. Polly brought me a warm mash that made me comfortable; and then they locked the door.

It was late the next morning before any one came, and then it was only Harry. He cleaned and fed us, and swept out the stalls; then he put the straw back again as if it was Sunday. He was very still, and neither whistled nor sang. At noon he came again and gave us our food and water; this time Dolly came with him. She was crying, and I could gather from what they said that Jerry was dangerously ill and the doctor said it was a bad case. So two days passed, and there was great trouble indoors. We saw only Harry and sometimes Dolly. I think she came for company, for Polly was always with Jerry, who had to be kept very quiet.

On the third day whilst Harry was in the stable, a tap came at the door, and Governor Grant came in.

'I wouldn't go to the house, my boy,' he said, 'but I want to know how your father is.'

'He is very bad,' said Harry, 'he can't be much worse. They call it bronchitis, and the doctor thinks it will turn one way or another to-night.'

'That's bad, very bad,' said Grant, shaking his head. 'I know two men who died of that last week. It takes 'em off in no time but whilst there's life there's hope, so you must keep up your spirits.'

'Yes,' said Harry quickly, 'and the doctor said that father had a better chance than most men, because he didn't drink. He said yesterday the fever was so high that if father had been a drinking man it would have burnt him up like a piece of paper; but I believe he thinks he will get over it; don't you think he will, Mr. Grant?'

The Governor looked puzzled.

'If there's any rule that good men should get over these things, I am sure he will, my boy. He's the best man I know. I'll look in early to-morrow.'

Early next morning he was there.

'Well?' said he.

'Father is better,' said Harry. 'Mother hopes he will get over it.'

'Thank God!' said the Governor; 'and now you must keep him warm, and keep his mind easy. And that brings me to the horses. You see, Jack will be all the better for a rest of a week or two in a warm stable, and you can easily take him a turn up and down the street to stretch his legs; but this young one, if he does not get work, will soon be all up on end as you may say, and will be rather too much for you; and when he does go out, there'll be an accident.'

'He is like that now,' said Harry; 'I have kept him short of corn, but he's so full of spirit I don't know what to do with him.'

'Just so,' said Grant. 'Now, look here. Will you tell your mother that, if she is agreeable, I will come for him every day till something is arranged, and take him for a good spell of work; and whatever he earns, I'll bring your mother half of it, and that will help with the horses' feed. Your father is in a good club, I know, but that won't keep the horses, and they'll be eating their heads off all this time; I'll come at noon to hear what she says;' and without waiting for Harry's thanks, he was gone.

At noon I think he went and saw Polly, for Harry and he came to the stable together, harnessed Hotspur, and took him out.

For a week or more he came for Hotspur, and when Harry thanked him or said anything about his kindness, he laughed it off, saying it was all good luck for him, for his horses were wanting a little rest, which they could not otherwise have had.

Jerry steadily grew better, but the doctor said that he must never go back to the cab-work again if he wished to be an old man. The children had many consultations together about what father and mother would do, and how they could help to earn money.

One afternoon Hotspur was brought in very wet and dirty.

'The streets are nothing but slush,' said the Governor; 'it will give you a good warming, my boy, to get him clean and dry.'

'All right, Governor,' said Harry, 'I shall not leave him till he is; you know I have been trained by my father.'

'I wish all the boys had been trained like you,' said the Governor.

While Harry was sponging off the mud from Hotspur's body and legs, Dolly came in, looking very full of something.

'Who lives at Fairstowe, Harry? Mother has got a letter from Fairstowe; she seemed so glad, and ran upstairs to father with it.'

'Don't you know? Why, it is the name of Mrs. Fowler's place—mother's old mistress, you know—the lady that father met last summer, who sent you and me five shillings each.'

'Oh! Mrs. Fowler; of course I know all about her. I wonder what she is writing to mother about.'

'Mother wrote to her last week,' said Harry. 'You know she told father if ever he gave up the cab-work, she would like to know. I wonder what she says; run in and see, Dolly.'

Harry scrubbed away at Hotspur with a 'huish! huish!' like any old ostler.

In a few minutes Dolly came dancing into the stable.

'Oh, Harry! was there ever anything so beautiful? Mrs. Fowler says we are all to go and live near her. There is a cottage now empty that will just suit us, with a garden, a hen-house, apple-trees, and everything! Her coachman is going away in the spring, and then she will want father in his place. And there are good families round, where you can get a place in the garden or stable, or as a page-boy; and there's a good school for me. Mother is laughing and crying by turns, and father does look so happy!'

'That's uncommon jolly,' said Harry, 'and just the right thing, I should say. It will suit father and mother both; but I don't intend to be a page-boy with tight clothes and rows of buttons. I'll be a groom or a gardener.'

It was quickly settled that, as soon as Jerry was well enough, they should remove to the country, and that the cab and horses should be sold as soon as possible.

This was heavy news for me, for I was not young now, and could not look for any improvement in my condition. Since I left Birtwick I had never been so happy as with my dear master Jerry; but three years of cab-work, even under the best conditions, will tell on one's strength, and I felt that I was not the horse that I had been.

Grant said at once that he would take Hotspur. There were men on the stand who would have bought me; but Jerry said I should not go to cab-work again with just anybody, and the Governor promised to find a place for me where I should be comfortable.

The day came for going away. Jerry had not been allowed to go out yet, and I never saw him after that New Year's Eve. Polly and the children came to bid me good-bye. 'Poor old Jack! dear old Jack! I wish we could take you with us,' she said; and then, laying her hand on my mane, she put her face close to my neck and kissed me. Dolly was crying, and she kissed me, too. Harry stroked me a great deal, but said nothing, only he seemed very sad; and so I was led away to my new place.

CHAPTER FORTY-SIX

JAKES AND THE LADY

I was sold to a corn dealer and baker whom Jerry knew, and with him he thought I should have good food and fair work. In the first he was quite right, and if my master had always been on the premises, I do not think I should have been overloaded; but there was a foreman who was always hurrying and driving every one, and frequently, when I had quite a full load, he would order something else to be taken on. My carter, whose name was Jakes, often said it was more than I ought to take, but the other always overruled him saying, "'Tis no use going twice when once will do, and I choose to get business forward.'

Jakes, like the other carters, always had the bearing rein up, which prevented me from drawing easily; and by the time I had been there three or four months, I found the work telling very much on my strength.

One day I was loaded more than usual, and part of the road was up a steep hill: I used all my strength, but I could not get on, and was obliged continually to stop. This did not please my driver, and he laid his whip on badly. 'Get on, you lazy fellow,' he said, 'or I'll make you.'

Again I started the heavy load, and struggled on a few yards; again the whip came down, and again I struggled forward. The pain of that great cart whip was sharp, but my mind was hurt quite as much as my poor sides. To be punished and abused when I was doing my very best was so hard that it took the heart out of me. A third time he was flogging me cruelly, when a lady stepped quickly up to him, and said in a sweet, earnest voice:—

'Oh! pray do not whip your good horse any more; I am sure he is doing all he can. The road is very steep, and I am sure he is doing his best.'

'If doing his best won't get this load up, he must do something more than his best; that's all I know, ma'am,' said Jakes.

'But is it not a very heavy load?' she said.

'Yes, yes, too heavy,' he said; 'but that's not my fault; the foreman came just as we were starting, and would have three hundredweight more put on to save him trouble. I must get on with it as well as I can.'

He was raising the whip again, when the lady said:—

'Pray, stop, I think I can help you if you will let me.'

The man laughed.

'You see,' she said, 'you do not give him a fair chance. He cannot use all his power with his head held back as it is with that bearing rein; if you would take it off, I am sure he would do better—*do* try it,' she said persuasively; 'I should be very glad if you would.'

'Well, well,' said Jakes, with a short laugh, 'anything to please a lady, of course. How far would you wish it down, ma'am?'

'Quite down; give him his head altogether.'

The rein was taken off, and in a moment I put my head down to my very knees. What a comfort it was! Then I tossed it up and down several times to get the aching stiffness out of my neck.

'Poor fellow! that is what you wanted,' said she, patting and stroking me with her gentle hand; 'and now if you will speak kindly to him and lead him on, I believe he will be able to do better.'

Jakes took the rein—'Come on, Blackie.' I put down my head, and threw my whole weight against the collar. I spared no strength; the load moved on, and I pulled it steadily up the hill, and then stopped to take breath.

The lady had walked along the footpath, and now came across into the road. She stroked and patted my neck, as I had not been patted for many a long day.

'You see, he was quite willing when you gave him the chance. I am sure he is a fine-tempered creature, and I daresay has known better days. You won't put that rein on again, will you?' for he was just going to hitch it up on the old plan.

'Well, ma'am, I can't deny that having his head has helped him up the hill, and I'll remember it another time, and thank you, ma'am; but if he went without a bearing rein I should be the laughing-stock of all the carters; it is the fashion, you see.'

'Is it not better,' she said, 'to lead a good fashion than to follow a bad one? A great many gentlemen do not use bearing reins now; our carriage horses have not worn them for fifteen years, and work with much less fatigue than those which have them; besides,' she added in a very serious voice, 'we have no right to distress any of God's creatures without a very good reason; we call them dumb animals, and so they are, for they cannot tell us how they feel, but they do not suffer less because they have no words. But I must not detain you now; I thank you for trying my plan with your good horse, and I am sure you will find it far better than the whip. Good-day.' And with another soft pat on my neck, she stepped lightly across the path, and I saw her no more.

'That was a real lady, I'll be bound for it,' said Jakes to himself; 'she spoke just as politely as if I was a gentleman. I'll try her plan, uphill, at any rate.'

I must do him the justice to say that he let my rein out

several holes, and after that, going uphill, he always gave me my head; but the heavy loads went on.

Good food and fair rest will keep up one's strength under full work, but no horse can stand against overloading; and I was getting so thoroughly pulled down from this cause that a younger horse was bought in my place. I may as well mention here what I suffered at this time from another cause. I had heard horses speak of it, but had never myself had experience of the evil of a badly-lighted stable. There was only one very small window at the end, and the consequence was that the stalls were almost dark.

Besides the depressing effect this had on my spirits, it very much weakened my sight, and when I was suddenly brought out of the darkness into the glare of daylight, it was very painful to my eyes. Several times I stumbled over the threshold, and could scarcely see where I was going.

I believe, had I stayed there very long, I should have become purblind, and that would have been a great misfortune; for I have heard men say that a stone-blind horse is safer to drive than one which has imperfect sight, as purblindness generally makes them very timid. However, I escaped without any permanent injury to my sight, and was sold to a large cab-owner.

CHAPTER FORTY-SEVEN

HARD TIMES

I SHALL never forget my new master. He had black eyes and a hooked nose; his mouth was as full of teeth as a bull-dog's, and his voice was as harsh as the grinding of cart wheels over gravel-stones. His name was Nicholas Skinner, and I believe he was the same man for whom poor Seedy Sam had driven.

I have heard men say that seeing is believing; but I should say that *feeling* is believing; for much as I had seen before, I never knew till now the utter misery of a cab-horse's life.

Skinner had a low set of cabs and a low set of drivers; he

was hard on the men, and the men were hard on the horses. In this place we had no Sunday rest, and it was in the heat of summer.

Sometimes on a Sunday morning a party of fast men would hire a cab for the day—four of them inside and another with the driver, and I had to take them ten or fifteen miles out into the country, and back again; never would any of them get down to walk up a hill, let it be ever so steep or the day ever so hot —unless indeed, when the driver was afraid I should not manage it, and sometimes I was so fevered and worn that I could hardly touch my food. How I used to long for the nice bran mash with nitre in it that Jerry used to give us on Saturday nights in hot weather, that used to cool us down and make us so comfortable. Then we had two nights and a whole day for unbroken rest, and on Monday morning we were as fresh as young horses again; but here there was no rest, and my driver was just as hard as his master.

He had a cruel whip with something so sharp at the end that it sometimes drew blood, and he would even whip me under the belly, and flip out the lash at my head. Indignities like these took the heart out of me terribly, but I still did my best and never hung back; for, as poor Ginger said, it was no use; men are the stronger.

My life was now so utterly wretched that I wished I might, like Ginger, drop down dead at my work, and so be out of my misery; and one day my wish very nearly came to pass.

I went on the stand at eight in the morning, and had done a good share of work when we had to take a fare to the railway. A long train was just expected in, so my driver pulled up at the back of some of the outside cabs to take the chance of a return fare. It was a very heavy train, and as all the cabs were soon engaged, ours was called for.

There was a party of four; a noisy, blustering man with a lady, a little boy, a young girl, and a great deal of luggage. The lady and the boy got into the cab, and while the man ordered about the luggage, the young girl came and looked at me.

'Papa,' she said, 'I am sure this poor horse cannot take us

and all our luggage so far; he is so very weak and worn out; do look at him.'

'Oh! he's all right, miss,' said my driver; 'he's strong enough.'

The porter, who was pulling about some heavy boxes, suggested to the gentleman that, as there was so much luggage, he should take a second cab.

'Can your horse do it, or can't he?' said the blustering man.

'Oh! he can do it all right sir. Send up the boxes, porter; he can take more than that.' Saying this, he helped to haul up a box so heavy that I could feel the springs go down.

'Papa, papa, do take a second cab,' said the young girl in a beseeching tone; 'I am sure we are wrong; I am sure it is very cruel.'

'Nonsense, Grace, get in at once, and don't make all this fuss; a pretty thing it would be if a man of business had to examine every cab-horse before he hired it—the man knows his own business of course; there, get in and hold your tongue!'

My gentle friend had to obey; and box after box was dragged up and lodged on top of the cab, or settled by the side of the driver. At last all was ready, and with his usual jerk of the rein and slash of the whip, he drove out of the station.

The load was very heavy, and I had had neither food nor rest since the morning; but I did my best, as I always had done in spite of cruelty and injustice.

I got along fairly till we came to Ludgate Hill; but there, the heavy load and my own exhaustion were too much. I was struggling to keep on, goaded by constant chucks of the rein and use of the whip, when, in a single moment—I cannot tell how—my feet slipped from under me, and I fell heavily to the ground on my side. The suddenness and the force with which I fell seemed to beat all the breath out of my body.

I lay perfectly still; indeed, I had no power to move, and I thought now I was going to die. I heard a sort of confusion round me—loud, angry voices, and the getting down of the luggage; but it was all like a dream. I thought I heard that sweet, pitiful voice saying, 'Oh! that poor horse! it is all our fault.'

Some one came and loosened the throat strap of my bridle,

and undid the traces which kept the collar so tight upon me. Some one said, 'He's dead; he'll never get up again.' Then I could hear a policeman giving orders, but I did not even open my eyes; I could only draw a gasping breath now and then. Some cold water was thrown over my head, some cordial was poured into my mouth, and something was covered over me.

I cannot tell how long I lay there, but I found my life coming back, and a kind-voiced man was patting me and encouraging me to rise. After some more cordial had been given me, and after one or two attempts, I staggered to my feet, and was gently led to some stables which were close by. Here I was put into a well-littered stall, and some warm gruel was brought to me; this I drank thankfully.

In the evening I was sufficiently recovered to be led back to Skinner's stables, where I think they did the best for me they could. In the morning Skinner came with a farrier to look at me. He examined me very closely, and said:—

'This is a case of overwork more than disease, and if you could give him a run off for six months, he would be able to work again; but now there is not an ounce of strength in him.'

'Then he must just go to the dogs,' said Skinner. 'I have no meadows to nurse sick horses in—he may get well or he may not; that sort of thing does not suit my business. My plan is to work 'em as long as they'll go, and then sell 'em for what they'll fetch at the knacker's or elsewhere.'

'If he was broken-winded,' said the farrier, 'you had better have had him killed out of hand, but he is not; there is a sale of horses coming off in about ten days; if you rest him and feed him up, he may pick up, and you may at any rate get more than his skin is worth.'

Upon this advice Skinner, rather unwillingly, I think, gave orders that I should be well fed and cared for; and the stable-man, happily for me, carried out the orders with a much better will than his master had shown in giving them.

Ten days of perfect rest, plenty of good oats, hay, and bran mashes with boiled linseed mixed in them, did more to get up my condition than anything else could have done. Those linseed mashes were delicious, and I began to think that after all it might be better to live than to go to the dogs. When the twelfth day after the accident came, I was taken to the sale, a few miles out of London. I felt that any change from my present place must be an improvement; so I held up my head, and hoped for the best.

CHAPTER FORTY-EIGHT

FARMER THOROUGHGOOD AND HIS GRANDSON WILLIE

AT this sale, of course, I found myself in company with the old broken-down horses—some lame, some broken-winded, some old, and some that I am sure it would have been merciful to shoot.

The buyers and sellers, too, many of them, looked not much better off than the poor beasts for which they were bargaining. There were poor old men trying to get a horse or pony for a few pounds to drag about some little wood or coal cart. There were poor men trying to sell a worn-out beast for two or three pounds, rather than have the greater loss of killing him.

Some of them looked as if poverty and hard times had hardened them all over; but there were others for whom I would willingly have used the last of my strength—poor and shabby, but kind and human, with voices that I could trust. There was one tottering old man that took a great fancy to me, and I to him, but I was not strong enough—it was an anxious time!

Coming from the better part of the fair, I noticed a man who looked like a gentleman farmer, with a young boy by his side. He had a broad back and round shoulders, a kind, ruddy face, and he wore a broad-brimmed hat. When he came up to me and my companions, he stood still and gave a pitiful look round upon us. I saw his eye rest on me; I had still a good mane and tail, which did something for my appearance. I pricked up my ears and looked at him.

'There's a horse, Willie, that has known better days.'

'Poor old fellow!' said the boy. 'Do you think, grandpapa, he was ever a carriage-horse?'

'Oh, yes, my boy,' said the farmer, coming closer, 'he might have been anything when he was young. Look at his nostrils and his ears, and the shape of his neck and shoulders; there's a deal of breeding about that horse.' He put out his hand and gave me a kind pat on the neck. I put out my nose in answer to his kindness, and the boy stroked my face.

'Poor old fellow! See, grandpapa, how well he understands kindness. Could you not buy him and make him young again, as you did Ladybird?'

'My dear boy, I can't make all old horses young. Besides, Ladybird was not so old as she was run down and badly used.'

'Well, grandpapa, I don't believe that this one is old; look at his mane and tail. I wish you would look into his mouth, and then you could tell. Though he is so very thin, his eyes are not sunken like some old horses.'

The old gentleman laughed. 'Bless the boy! he is as horsy as his old grandfather.'

'But do look at his mouth, grandpapa, and ask the price; I am sure he would grow young in our meadows.'

The man who had brought me for sale now put in his word.

'The young gentleman's a real knowing one, sir. Now the fact is, this 'ere hoss is just pulled down with overwork in the cabs. He's not an old one, and I heard as how the vet. should say that a six months' run off would set him right up, being as how his wind was not broken. I've had the tending of him these ten days past, and a more grateful and pleasant animal I never met. 'Twould be worth a gentleman's while to give a five-pound note for him and let him have a chance. I'll be bound he'd be worth twenty pounds next spring.'

The old gentleman laughed, and the little boy looked up eagerly.

'Oh! grandpapa, did you not say the colt sold for five pounds more than you expected? You would not be poorer if you did buy this one.'

The farmer slowly felt my legs, which were much swollen

and strained; then he looked at my mouth—'Thirteen or fourteen, I should say. Just trot him out, will you?'

I arched my poor thin neck, raised my tail a little, and threw out my legs as well as I could, for they were very stiff.

'What is the lowest you will take for him?' said the farmer as I came back.

'Five pounds, sir; that was the lowest price my master set.'

''Tis a speculation,' said the old gentleman, shaking his head, but at the same time slowly drawing out his purse—'quite a speculation! Have you any more business here?' he said, counting the sovereigns into the man's hand.

'No, sir, I can take him for you to the inn if you please.'

'Do so; I am now going there.'

They walked forward, and I was left behind. The boy could hardly control his delight, and the old gentleman seemed to enjoy his pleasure. I had a good feed at the inn, and was then gently ridden home by a servant of my new master and turned into a large meadow with a shed in one corner of it.

Mr. Thoroughgood, for that was the name of my benefactor, gave orders that I should have hay and oats every night and morning, and the run of the meadow during the day. 'You, Willie,' said he, 'must take the oversight of him; I give him into your charge.'

The boy was proud of his charge, and undertook it in all seriousness. There was not a day when he did not pay me a visit, picking me out from among the other horses to give me a bit of carrot or some other good thing, or sometimes to stand by me whilst I ate my oats. He always came with kind words and caresses, and of course I grew very fond of him. He called me Old Crony, as I used to come to him in the field and follow him about. Sometimes he brought his grandfather, who always looked closely at my legs.

'That is our point, Willie,' he would say; 'but he is improving so steadily that I think we shall see a change for the better in the spring.'

The perfect rest, the good food, the soft turf, and gentle exercise soon began to tell on my condition and my spirits. I had a good constitution from my mother, and I was never strained when I was young, so that I had a better chance than many horses who have been worked before they came to their full strength.

During the winter my legs improved so much that I began to feel quite young again. The spring came round, and one day in March Mr. Thoroughgood determined that he would try me in the phaeton. I was well pleased, and he and Willie drove me a few miles. My legs were not stiff now, and I did the work with perfect ease.

'He's growing young, Willie; we must give him a little gentle work now, and by midsummer he will be as good as Ladybird; he has a beautiful mouth and good paces; these could not be better.'

'Oh, grandpapa, how glad I am you bought him!'

'So am I, my boy, but he has to thank you more than me. We must now be looking out for a quiet, genteel place for him where he will be valued.'

CHAPTER FORTY-NINE

MY LAST HOME

ONE day during the summer the groom cleaned and dressed me with such extraordinary care that I thought some new change must be at hand. He trimmed my fetlocks and legs, passed the tarbrush over my hoofs, and even parted my forelock. I think the harness also had an extra polish. Willie seemed half anxious, half merry, and he got into the chaise with his grandfather.

'If the ladies take to him,' said the old gentleman, 'they'll be suited, and he'll be suited; we can but try.'

At the distance of a mile or two from the village we came to a pretty low house with a lawn and shrubbery at the front and a drive up to the door. Willie rang the bell, and asked if Miss Blomefield or Miss Ellen was at home. Yes, they both were. So whilst Willie stayed with me, Mr. Thoroughgood went into the house.

In about ten minutes he returned, followed by three ladies.

One tall, pale lady, wrapped in a white shawl, leaned on a younger lady with dark eyes and a merry face; the third, a very stately-looking person, was Miss Blomefield. They all came to look at me and ask questions. The younger lady—this was Miss Ellen—took to me very much; she said she was sure she should like me, for I had such a good face. The tall, pale lady said that she should always be nervous in riding behind a horse that had once been down, as I might come down again; and if I did, she should never get over the fright.

'You see, ladies,' said Mr. Thoroughgood, 'many first-rate horses have their knees broken through the carelessness of their drivers, without any fault of their own; and from what I see of this horse, I should say that is his case; but of course I do not wish to influence you. If you wish, you can have him on trial, and then your coachman will see what he thinks of him.'

'You have always been such a good adviser to us about our horses,' said the stately lady, 'that your recommendation would go a long way with me, and if my sister Lavinia sees no objection, we will accept with thanks your offer of a trial.'

It was then arranged that I should be sent for the next day.

In the morning a smart-looking young man came for me. At first he looked pleased, but when he saw my knees, he said in a disappointed voice: 'I didn't think, sir, you would have recommended my ladies a blemished horse like this.'

'Handsome is that handsome does,' said my master. 'You are only taking him on trial, and I am sure you will do fairly by him, young man; and if he is not as safe as any horse you ever drove, send him back.'

I was led home, placed in a comfortable stable, fed, and left to myself. The next day, when my groom was cleaning my face, he said: 'That is just like the star that Black Beauty had, and he is much the same height, too; I wonder where he is now.'

A little farther on he came to the place in my neck where I was bled, and where a little knot was left in the skin. He almost started, and began to look me over carefully, talking to himself.

'White star in the forehead, one white foot on the off side, this little knot just in that place;' then looking at the middle of my back—'and as I am alive, there is that little patch of white hair that John used to call "Beauty's threepenny-bit." It *must* be Black Beauty! Why, Beauty! Beauty! do you know me, little Joe Green that almost killed you?' And he began patting and patting me as if he was quite overjoyed.

I could not say that I remembered him, for now he was a fine grown young fellow with black whiskers and a man's voice, but I was sure he knew me, and that he was Joe Green; so I was very glad. I put my nose up to him, and tried to say that we were friends. I never saw a man so pleased.

'Give him a fair trial! I should think so indeed! I wonder who the rascal was that broke your knees, my old Beauty! You must have been badly served out somewhere. Well, well, it won't be my fault if you haven't good times of it now. I wish John Manly were here to see you.'

In the afternoon I was put into a low-park chair and brought to the door. Miss Ellen was going to try me, and Green went with her. I soon found that she was a good driver, and she seemed pleased with my paces. I heard Joe telling her about me, and that he was sure I was Squire Gordon's old Black Beauty.

When we returned, the other sisters came out to hear how I had behaved myself. She told them what she had just heard, and said, 'I shall certainly write to Mrs. Gordon to tell her that her favourite horse has come to us. How pleased she will be!'

After this I was driven every day for a week or so, and as I appeared to be quite safe, Miss Lavinia at last ventured out in the small close carriage. After this, it was quite decided to keep me and to call me by my old name of 'Black Beauty.'

I have now lived in this happy place a whole year. Joe is the best and kindest of grooms. My work is easy and pleasant, and I feel my strength and spirits all coming back again. Mr. Thoroughgood said to Joe the other day, 'In your place he will last till he is twenty years old—perhaps more.'

Willie always speaks to me when he can, and treats me as his special friend. My ladies have promised that I shall never be sold, and so I have nothing to fear; and here my story ends. My troubles are all over and I am at home; and often before I am quite awake I fancy I am still in the orchard at Birtwick, standing with my old friends under the apple-trees.